W9-CMP-697

WITHDRAWN

# DOUBLE SWITCH

Also by T. T. Monday

*The Setup Man*

# DOUBLE SWITCH

A NOVEL

## T. T. MONDAY, 1976-

Doubleday
*New York London Toronto*
*Sydney Auckland*

This is a work of fiction. Names, characters, places, and
incidents either are the product of the author's imagination
or are used fictitiously. Any resemblance to actual persons,
living or dead, events, or locales is entirely coincidental.

Copyright © 2016 by Nick Taylor

All rights reserved. Published in the United States by Doubleday,
a division of Penguin Random House LLC, New York, and
distributed in Canada by Random House of Canada,
a division of Penguin Random House Canada Ltd., Toronto.

www.doubleday.com

DOUBLEDAY and the portrayal of an anchor with a dolphin are
registered trademarks of Penguin Random House LLC.

*Jacket illustration: ball © Nikita Chisnikov/Shutterstock;
bullet holes © sugardragon/Shutterstock.com
Jacket design Michael Windsor*

Library of Congress Cataloging-in-Publication Data
Monday, T. T., [date]
Double switch : a novel / T. T. Monday. — First edition.
pages ; cm
ISBN 978-0-385-53995-1 (hardcover)
ISBN 978-0-385-53996-8 (eBook)
I. Title.
PS3620.A95945D68 2016
813'.6—dc23
2015029322

MANUFACTURED IN THE UNITED STATES OF AMERICA

1 3 5 7 9 10 8 6 4 2

First Edition

*For Paul Taylor, an old southpaw*

# DOUBLE SWITCH

# 1

The girl reporter stands outside the bullpen gate. She's wearing a coral sleeveless jumper, belted at the waist, with vertical pleats that wink open across the chest. Yellow curls fall on suntanned shoulders. A laminated identification card hangs on a lanyard around her neck. All the regional cable networks now have on-field correspondents, usually young women, who interview players and coaches between innings for a little added color. In my experience, they are polite and knowledgeable about the game, but my experience is limited. Field reporters tend to have little interest in relief pitchers.

"Dugout's that way," I holler through the gate. Here in San José, the bullpens are behind the outfield fence, three hundred feet from the rest of the team. This is where I spend my time, working through buckets of sunflower seeds with the other relievers, waiting for the manager to call. Tonight's game ended half an hour ago, and the concrete floor under the bullpen bench is covered in seed hulls, tobacco spit, and trampled Gatorade cups. The crowd has gone home. My teammates are down in the clubhouse, dressing for the flight to Denver. We start a three-game series against the Rockies tomorrow afternoon. I will join them in a minute, but first I'm enjoying a moment of peace and quiet. An empty bullpen is the closest thing I have to an office.

The reporter smiles. She has straight teeth and shallow blue eyes—pretty, but not stopping traffic. She looks familiar, even though I'm sure we haven't met. She must be with the visiting club.

"Adcock, right? May I come in?"

"Where's the camera guy?"

"No camera tonight. I just need some quotes."

I look at the clock on the scoreboard. "I can give you five minutes."

"That will be plenty of time, thanks."

I open the gate. Her perfume is light and fruity, citrus with a hint of musk. She ducks under my arm. "You're the detective, right?"

I pull the gate closed but don't respond right away. Over the last decade I've developed a reputation for solving problems. Players come to me with cheating wives, gambling debts—issues that need resolution but which they'd prefer not to take to the police. Sometimes the work is easy. Sometimes all it takes is a couple of phone calls. A couple of times it's almost taken my life. One morning last season, while my teammates were taping their ankles and stretching out their hamstrings in an air-conditioned major-league clubhouse, I was on my knees in a warehouse in Tijuana, facing the dark asshole of a nine-millimeter pistol. I thought I was punched out for sure, but I lived. Didn't even miss the game.

My services aren't just for players. I've helped coaches, clubhouse guys, even a couple of front-office personnel. Never a TV reporter, though.

"Am I the detective? I guess that depends who's asking."

"I'm Tiff Tate." She puts out her right hand.

I pause. "The stylist?"

"We had to meet eventually, don't you think?"

Tiff Tate is a major operator behind the scenes in Major League Baseball, right up there with the superagents and the major-market GMs. In exchange for a fee rumored to be in the mid–six figures, Tiff designs a custom on-field look for each of her clients, making recommendations on everything from uniform styling and grooming to the song that plays when he walks up to bat. In an era when star athletes can earn several times their annual salary in endorsements, Tiff was one of the first consultants to recognize the primacy of an athlete's image, the importance of building a unique and marketable persona. She works hand in glove with the companies her clients endorse; in fact, many of her clients come to her through contacts at apparel companies. In Boston, where she is based, she created the original Caveman look for Johnny Damon and helped David Ortiz upgrade his jewelry from a cross on a skinny chain to the ropy bling you now see him wearing in postgame interviews. Lately she has been focusing her practice on beards. I've been told she was the architect of the "Fear the Beard" campaign that propelled Brian Wilson and the Giants to the 2010 World Series title. The year before, Wilson had been a good-but-not-great closer with a balky right arm and pretty eyes. After consulting with Tiff Tate, he was the heart of a championship club. Her work is legendary, lucrative, and highly confidential. Few players admit to using her services, but it's not hard to guess who they are.

"When did you become a reporter?" I ask.

"You mean this?" She lifts the laminated ID off her chest. The name reads AMANDA HUTCHINS. "This is just my ticket to the bullpen."

"I wasn't aware you needed a ticket."

She shrugs. "I wanted to meet you—and I've never tried the reporter look." She lays her head back and shakes out her mane. "So far I like it."

"Well, I'm grateful that you made the effort, but I'm happy with my look."

In a glance, she sizes me up: a thirty-six-year-old white man, six two and 190 pounds. Slate-colored eyes, straight nose, a hint of gray at the temples. No facial hair. No jewelry of any kind, not even a tan line from a wedding ring (that faded years ago). White baseball pants loose to the ankles. Blue undershirt. San José Bay Dogs jersey number 39.

"What I mean to say is, thanks, but I don't need you."

"Right," she comes back, "I need you."

"How's that?"

"Did I forget the code word? My understanding is that you solve problems."

"I used to." It's June, two and a half months into the season, and I haven't worked a case all year. I've had plenty of inquiries, mostly matrimonial work, but I've turned them all down. My appetite for cheating wives has vanished. There's no mystery to it: the owner of the aforementioned nine was a player's wife.

"You can talk," I say, "but I'm not promising anything."

Tiff Tate nods. "It's about Yonel Ruiz."

Now she has my attention. Ruiz, the Colorado Rockies' rookie outfielder, is the story of the year, a Cuban defector who escaped the island in a Zodiac powerboat, hidden under a tarp with a couple of political refugees and a Santería priest. Just making land was a triumph, but Ruiz has done more than that. He's absolutely crushing the ball, on pace to hit thirty-five homers and drive in 120 runs in his first major-league season. He also steals bases at will and cuts down runners from right field like an army sniper. So far, no opposing pitcher has figured him out. The scouting line is nothing more than wishful thinking. The man swings the bat like a maniac, like each plate appearance could be his last. Which makes sense, given what he's been through.

Cuba is hemorrhaging ballplayers. The real exodus started in the early nineties, after the Soviet Union fell apart and the island became desperately poor. As I remember it, the first defectors to make a serious impact in the major leagues were Liván Hernández and his brother Orlando, aka "El Duque." With their All-Star résumés and paychecks full of zeroes, Liván and El Duque inspired other Cubans to make the leap. The trickle became a flood, and now it seems like every club has one or two on the roster. The Tigers' All-Star left fielder is *cubano,* as is the White Sox's first baseman, the Reds' closer, and half the Yankees' rotation. It's hard to believe there are any talented players left in Havana. Major League Baseball has been lobbying in Washington to have the visa rules relaxed, or at least to have ballplayers separated from cigars and other Cuban produce regulated by the trade embargo. The current compromise requires that clubs pay a luxury tax if they exceed a spending cap on Cuban players. Bidding wars have driven salaries to eight figures with mind-blowing frequency. Then again, guys like José Abreu, Aroldis Chapman, and Yonel Ruiz keep delivering the goods. I hesitate to use the word "obsessed," but I've been following the Cuban thing very closely, as have most American players.

"I'm listening," I say.

"Can I assume this conversation is confidential?"

I toe the dirt. "Sure, why not?"

"Yonel's people came to see me about six months ago. This was right after he arrived in the U.S. I told them I would do a consultation, but they had to respect my rules. The sessions had to be private, just me and him. No managers or agents in the room."

"They wanted to watch?"

"I have to protect my intellectual property. If I let them watch, I'd have Scott Boras on the phone asking for the same privilege."

"You can't have that."

"Not at all. So I met with Yonel, and he turned out to be a real pleasure. His style presented itself right away, a kind of Caribbean night horse with MMA appeal. Chin beard, zircon studs, Hong Kong gangster ink . . ." She ticks off the menu on the fingers of her left hand.

I picture the muscle-bound slugger in the batter's box, coiled arms heaving, sweat glistening on his sharp facial hair. "You did well," I say.

"Thanks. With most of my clients, I have monthly check-ins where I perform adjustments, maybe add a piercing or change the color of the undershirt, that sort of thing. You need to evolve the look. Anyway, during one of these visits Yonel asks if he can tell me something. He has these really dark, sad eyes. . . ."

"'Sad' isn't the word I'd use. But okay."

"He tells me he's being blackmailed by the Venezuelans who smuggled him out of Cuba."

"Venezuelans, huh?"

"They control the Caribbean smuggling racket."

"I've heard it's lucrative."

"What else have you heard?"

"Just that it costs an arm and a leg to get off the island, and that half the time you get caught by the Coast Guard or the Cuban authorities, and there are no refunds or rain checks."

The previous winter, after Ruiz established residency in Mexico, the Rockies signed him for six years and fifty million dollars—at the time the largest deal ever for a Cuban defector. Everyone said it was a foolish move for the club. Now the same people are saying Ruiz should have held out for more.

"Honestly," I say, "if clubs weren't paying these guys so much, we wouldn't have this problem."

Tiff eyes me. "His family is being held at gunpoint in Havana. As soon as Ruiz signed the contract, the Venezuelans seized them as collateral. They've been unable to leave the house for months."

"What's the ransom?"

"Originally it was a million, then they raised it to five, then ten, then twenty. Eventually, they decided to take it all."

"But it's a six-year deal," I say. "He doesn't get the whole amount up front."

"They know that. They're asking him to have his salary paid into an account they control. They already take his endorsement money that way."

"How do they expect him to live?"

"He'll have an allowance. Enough to keep up appearances."

"Did they set an ultimatum?"

"Two weeks. If they don't get confirmation from the bank next payday, they start shooting the family. They have his parents, his siblings, his wife, their little daughter. . . ." She's upset, maybe more upset than you'd expect a consultant to be over a client's personal troubles.

"Help me understand," I say. "You're here out of the goodness of your heart?"

"Yonel is a friend. Have you ever helped a friend?"

"So why didn't he come to see me himself? Everyone in baseball knows what I do."

"He can't. He isn't allowed to speak with anyone outside the Rockies organization—no reporters, no fans, not even players from other teams. The only person he's allowed to see privately is me, and that's only because the smugglers are convinced that they need me in order to maximize their investment."

"You know I don't have any strings to pull with the Venezuelan Mafia."

"Of course not. I just need you to find them."

"Ruiz must know who they are."

Tiff shakes her head slowly. "These guys are sophisticated. It's a blind hierarchy all the way to the top. The men in the Zodiac boat hand you off to operatives on the shore in Mexico, who give you to the immigration expediters, and so on. At some point you pass over into the legitimate world. Yonel's agent is with IMG."

"The agent is involved?"

"Not directly. The Venezuelans pass him messages through a go-between. The shepherds in the U.S. never show themselves. Yonel gets calls from untraceable numbers, unsigned notes in his hotel room."

"Can I see the notes?"

Tiff frowns, as though it hadn't occurred to her that I might want to examine the evidence. "I'll ask Yonel to bring them next time we meet."

"Tell me more about the phone calls. Is that how he received the threat about his family?"

"I think so. I mean, that's how they communicate."

Something doesn't feel right here. God knows I'm sympathetic to Ruiz's situation, but if I were in trouble that deep, there's no way I would trust my salvation to a stylist with a vague grasp on the facts.

I can't decide how I feel about Tiff Tate. On the one hand, she's obviously in the snake-oil game. Monthly fine-tuning for a beard and advice on how to wear your pants? Who is she kidding? She's exploiting ballplayers every bit as much as these Venezuelan coyotes. And she's a liar—or at least she's comfortable doing business in a disguise. On the other hand, I like her attitude. Most people, ordinary citizens, regard Major

League Baseball with a reverence bordering on foolishness. They believe an institution so old and storied must be honest at its core. Even after the '94 strike, even after steroids, they continue to believe. Baseball is the drunken uncle America keeps inviting back to Thanksgiving, even though we know he's going to puke and pass out on the floor. I like that Tiff isn't averting her eyes.

"Call the police," I tell her. "As long as Ruiz is here legally, I don't see any reason they couldn't help him out."

"The police? You think the Denver police can just push their way into Cuba and fix this?"

"Not the Denver police. I'm talking about FBI, ICE, one of those federal agencies."

Tiff pushes out her jaw. "Maybe Yonel was right."

"About what?"

"We should have called Jim Feldspar."

Feldspar is Major League Baseball's new Director of Personnel Security, a position created last off-season by the commissioner's office, ostensibly to assist players in their dealings with the law—and also, I have to believe, to keep an eye on us. Feldspar is a former player whose pro career fizzled out in the minors. That's usually the beginning of a sad biography ending with an hourly job in a sporting-goods store, but Feldspar reinvented himself after baseball. He joined the Secret Service and spent twenty years protecting presidents and their families before circling back to his first vocation. We've never met, but I have his number on the back of my stadium keycard, placed there by the clubhouse staff during spring training, on a sticker with the innocuous label MLB HELPLINE. Rumor has it that, in the few months Feldspar has been on the job, he has already hushed up half a dozen DUIs and at least one concealed-weapons charge. Nice work, if it's true.

"You can still call him," I say, trying to play it cool. Truth is, I feel threatened by Feldspar. I won't be able to pitch forever. Investigations are my retirement plan. The game isn't big enough for two fixers.

"I convinced him to try you first."

"You don't know me from Adam."

"Well, like I told Yonel, I'm sure someone in the league office would be happy to advise him on how to wear his pants, but that doesn't mean they have his best interests in mind."

"Who says I do?"

"I can give you a week. After that we'll have to call Feldspar."

"Suppose I find these guys—then what? I don't do hits."

"Who said anything about killing?" Tiff laughs. "Just find them. I'll take it from there." She looks me in the eye and holds the stare until she's sure I understand. Then she hands me her card and leaves the bullpen.

# 2

When the charter touches down in Denver, I receive a text from Erik Magnusson, a former teammate now working as the Rockies' hitting coach. If there's anyone on the Colorado payroll willing to give me an honest perspective on Yonel Ruiz, it's Magnusson. He suggests we meet for a drink at Joey's Big Sky, a bar near the team hotel. Although it's one in the morning, I text back to say I can meet if he's still up. Magnusson says sure, he could use a break from the video room.

Joey's Big Sky is equal parts John Ford and Santa Claus. The bones of the place are classic Old West: rough-sawn plank floors and walls, dark rafters, lazy ceiling fans. Taxidermied heads of bison, moose, and antelope are installed above the bar, draped in tinsel and electric candy-cane lights even though it's June. A billiard table covered in stained green felt sits unused under a rusty can light. The only patrons at this hour are serious drunks, hunched reverently over rail whiskeys and watery domestic beer. Magnusson sticks out not only because he's drinking soda, but because he appears to be the only man in the room who could run a quarter-mile without dropping dead. Erect on the stool, Magnusson looks like a well-kept golf pro, lats bulging under his polo. Magnusson was a slugger—never a Gold Glover, but a capable left fielder looking forward to a long twilight as a DH until his name turned up in the Mitchell Report in 2007. He claimed innocence, but so did everyone named in the report, including near-certain dopers like Canseco, Bonds, and Giambi. The Bay Dogs cut him loose, and no other club would take a chance. He couldn't even get work in Japan. He was tainted, a cheater. Fortunately for Magnusson, memories are short in baseball, and a year ago the Rockies called with the coaching offer.

For what it's worth, I always believed him. I even lobbied our GM to give him another chance. Looking at him now, I feel vindicated. I want to take a picture and send it to Senator Mitchell himself. See that? Erik Magnusson isn't taking steroids in retirement, and he still looks like the Incredible Hulk.

When Magnusson sees me, he stands and holds out a hand as deep as a first baseman's glove. "Long time no see, buddy."

I order a beer. Magnusson takes a refill of Sprite.

He looks around. None of the drunks lift their heads. When our drinks arrive, we pick them up and move to a booth in the back. The walls are covered with etched phone numbers and misspelled obscenities. The tabletop is sticky with God knows what. Big Erik Magnusson lumbers onto the bench.

"So you want to know about Ruiz," he says.

"I was going to ask about your family first."

"He's a hell of a player, hits for average and power, good plate discipline, lots of walks for someone his age. A nice inside-out swing, keeps the bat level . . ." He pauses, and his voice drops an octave. "Because you're my friend, I'm going to be honest with you. Stay away from Ruiz."

"Why? What's the matter with him?"

Mags takes a long pull on his Sprite and shakes his head. He does not elaborate.

"I trust you, Mags, but you're gonna have to give me more than that. Tell me who he hangs out with, at least."

"Short answer? Nobody. He speaks with no one, and he hangs around with no one. He shows up, he plays, and he leaves."

"Come on. There are two other Cubans on the team—the third baseman, Oliva, and what's the other guy's name, the righty reliever?"

"Cabrera."

"Yeah. Ruiz talks to them, right?"

"Not that I've seen."

"Okay . . . so he's quiet. How does that translate to 'stay away at all costs'?"

"You're working a case, aren't you?" Magnusson looks me dead in the eye, like he's about to tell me something; then he exhales and leans back. "You want to know about the family? Things are not good. Patti left me in February, right before spring training. Out of nowhere she announces that she's in love with this woman Brenda, a trainer at the gym. Pretty lady—I know who she is—never would have guessed she was a lesbian." He pauses. "Guess I could say the same thing about Patti. Anyway, I feel like a moron. Then she tells me she and Brenda are moving to Palm Desert, and of course they're taking the kids. Our kids. Which means it will be pretty much impossible for me to visit on off days, and, besides that, it sucks for the kids, because they're already in high school. Who moves their kids in the middle of high school to go live in the desert? It's so selfish. . . ." I notice that his fists are balled up. "It makes me crazy. Sorry."

"You have every right to be pissed."

"Sometimes I wonder if it's my fault. I wasn't around all those years, and then, when I finally was, I just stormed around the house with a chip on my shoulder, all angry about the doping thing. I should have paid more attention to her. On the other hand, Patti says she didn't just turn gay. She says she always was, which I find hard to believe."

"It's not your fault. You did the best you could. You were providing for your family."

Magnusson shrugs, and his brow stacks up with wrinkles. "How do you handle it? You've been divorced how long?"

"Thirteen years. We split when Isabel was a baby. She'll be a sophomore in high school this fall."

"Your ex lives in L.A., right?"

"Santa Monica."

"We're in Scottsdale . . . or we were."

"I could tell you that you'll get over it, but that's not exactly right. You will move on. And you will see your kids. Christmas break, I took Izzy skiing."

"I've thought of that, but I really don't want to be that guy. You know, the divorced dad who takes his kids on fancy vacations once a year but otherwise doesn't see them?"

"Well, you're divorced, and you're a dad. Those are the facts. The rest is up to you."

"That's helpful." Magnusson rattles the ice in his glass.

I think about how to steer the conversation back to Ruiz. As much as I'd like to continue this therapy session, we're playing a matinee tomorrow. Today, rather.

"So—Yonel Ruiz," Magnusson says, unprompted. "He lived with me for a week before spring training."

"Wait—he lived with you?"

"I was alone in this big house, so, when the front office asked around for someone to put Ruiz up for a few days, I said sure. He moved into our guest room, and he was nice enough, always cleaned up in the kitchen and asked before using the computer. We didn't speak much."

"What did he do on the computer?"

"Mostly video calls with his family, checking e-mail, that sort of thing."

"Any artifacts?"

"Artifacts?"

"Downloads, chat conversations, maybe he left his e-mail open?"

"You think I spied on him?"

"You might have been curious, I don't know. . . ."

"Hey, you're the detective, not me. And, besides, at that point I had no reason to suspect him of anything."

"But later on you did?"

"Like I said, he only stayed with me for a week. After that he moved into his own place. But then, the night before the season began—my last day in Arizona—I got a phone call. It was an anonymous caller, disguised voice and all that, like on *60 Minutes.* The guy says I'm forbidden to speak with anyone about Yonel Ruiz. If I wanted to live, I'd keep my mouth shut. That's what he said."

"Keep your mouth shut about what?"

Mags shakes his head. "No idea."

This doesn't make sense. No extortionist would make a threat so vague.

"He must have had something in mind. Did you overhear anything, maybe in the video calls with Ruiz's family?"

"I don't speak Spanish."

I give Mags my 3-2 stare. "What did you say to the caller?"

"I said I'd keep my mouth shut about Ruiz. And I have, until now."

"Erik, I'd love to take a look at your computer, the one Ruiz used."

"Too late for that. As soon as I got that call, I reformatted the hard drive. I took it down to the Apple Store and told them to wipe it clean. I didn't want anything to do with him."

The light above the booth flickers, then comes back on. I look over to the bar. The regulars are shifting on their stools. Closing time.

"Tell me more about the call. Did you get a read on the voice?"

"It was one of those computerized robot voices, like in a dance song."

A robot singer. What the hell am I supposed to do with that? "Any idea who it might have been?"

Mags shakes his head. "Somebody who hates Ruiz, I guess. I feel bad for him. I know what he went through to get here. Those island boys grow up in mud, and now he has to contend with threats over here? I wish I could give you more."

"No, this was good. I appreciate you taking the time to meet me."

The sidewalk is surprisingly lively at 2:00 a.m. Joey's Big Sky is in a district with a lot of other bars, and they're all closing up, spilling dozens of patrons into the street. A couple of girls in heels and Lycra stride up between Mags and me. They ask where we're going next.

"Back to work," Magnusson says.

"What kind of work?" says the prettier of the two. She smiles impishly at Magnusson. It occurs to me that he might not know they're on the job.

"I watch video of the men I supervise and give them instructions on how to improve their job performance."

"You watch videos. So you're a security guard?"

Magnusson laughs and turns to me. "What do you think? Could I be a security guard?"

In my mind, anything would be preferable to Magnusson's job. Hitting instructors work crazy hours, and the pressure is enormous. Magnusson has told me he's in the video room every morning at seven, and after the game he's there till midnight or one, analyzing the at-bats of every underperforming position player. He watches their swings, frame by frame, looking for mechanical problems. The tiniest adjustment in elbow height can alter the plane of the swing, leading to more contact, better contact, whatever the player needs. Maybe the player is planting his foot too early or dropping his trailing hand too late. There's a checklist. I have to believe most hitting instructors are hoping to be promoted within a couple of years to a better role, like first-base coach. I can't imagine watching video longer than that. My eyes would burn out.

"My friend here has been working too hard," I say.

The prettier of the two hookers has watery blue eyes and pale skin. Feather tattoos on both arms. "We're just like him," she says. "Working all the time."

"Work, work, work," her partner says, pouting. "No time to play."

"Hey, I have an idea! How about you knock off early tonight and have some fun off the clock? My buddy could use some company."

The whores look at each other, then at the rapidly thinning crowd. The pretty one says, "You two have a good night," and she takes her friend by the arm. They run off on wobbly heels, calling after a couple of men in business suits.

I turn to Magnusson. "Are you really headed back to work?"

"Have to," he says. "Anglin was one for seventeen last week, two for twenty the week before that. It's a real predicament he's in." Dan Anglin is the Rockies' first baseman, a former All-Star the Rockies claimed for peanuts last winter. He surprised everyone in baseball by getting hot in April and May, reminding us how it used to be. The talk was about how shrewd the Colorado front office had been, finding a seaworthy vessel where others had seen a rotting hull. Then, this month, he cooled off. Now people are saying he might be finished. Magnusson is probably Anglin's last chance. That's a big weight for a coach to carry.

"Have you found anything?"

Magnusson looks at his watch. "It's two o'clock in the morning and I'm headed back to the clubhouse. What do you think?"

I want to continue our conversation. I still have questions about Ruiz. "Meet me for breakfast. You know the Starbucks across from the main gate? Be there at nine."

"Nine?"

"There's a couch in the video room. Take a nap."

"A nap? I'm forty-two years old!"

"Those are baseball years, Mags. On the scale of human maturity, you're still a toddler."

# 3

Next morning I text Bil Chapman, the Bay Dogs' clubhouse manager, to tell him I won't be on the bus to the park. He texts back a three-second clip from a porn film—the last three seconds of the action, if you follow me. The annotation reads: "This is you last night I bet!" Bil is forty-three, and those are clubhouse-guy years, the worst kind of arrested development. When he's not traveling with the team, Bil lives at home with his mother.

A cab drops me in front of Coors Field. It's not yet 9:00 a.m., and fans are already lining up. These days, most major-league parks allow the public to watch batting practice, and the altitude in Denver has enabled the Rockies to make BP an event. Three hours before game time, the line stretches down the block. Kids with baseball gloves are bouncing on their toes, arguing with one another about the best spot in the bleachers to catch home runs. Their moms and dads chase after them with sunscreen. It's an aw-shucks moment, a Norman Rockwell painting, just the kind of thing the commissioner's office wants the world to see. I remember being one of those kids, waiting for the gates to open on Sunday morning at Dodger Stadium. My dad would bring his three-inch-thick Sunday

*Los Angeles Times,* and I had my glove, a stack of baseball cards, and a Sharpie. For me it was the happiest place on earth—better than Disneyland, and cheaper, too.

I order a coffee and take a seat. Seeing myself in those kids makes me sad. Now I know it was all a farce. As I roamed the bleachers in thrall, my heroes were in the clubhouse popping pills and corking their bats. The sport has cleaned up since then, but baseball is and has always been a cheater's game. Twenty years from now, we'll look back on today's game and wonder why we didn't realize that it was all fixed, that computers had predicted the outcome of every game. Or why we didn't recognize that the Cubans were genetically engineering players. It won't be the first time Major League Baseball has pulled the wool over the eyes of fans. In the 1960s and '70s, the players were jacked on amphetamines. Greenies, dexies, ephedrine, "players' coffee." The public had no idea.

So there I am, contemplating the vast hypocrisy that pays my salary, when I realize I've finished my coffee. It's nine-twenty, and Magnusson still hasn't shown. I call his cell and get voice mail. I imagine him passed out on the sofa in the video room, oblivious to the vibrations in his pocket. Let's hope he found the flaw in Dan Anglin's swing, at least.

Then the police arrive. I hear the sirens first, the noise reflected off the stone stadium façade. Three cruisers squeal into the loading zone and park at jagged angles. They kill the sirens but leave the red-and-blue strobes pulsing. Half a dozen uniformed officers leap out. The kids on line stop bouncing; the parents put away their sunscreen and newspapers. They all just stare.

I toss my cup in the trash and leave the shop. A lump forms in my throat, but I swallow it down. Couldn't be.

I jog around back, to the players' entrance, and show my ID

to the guard on the stool. I ask if he knows anything about the police out front.

"Police? Like, DPD, or just security?"

"Police," I repeat. "Three squad cars, with sirens and lights. You didn't hear it?"

"Nope," the guard says.

I don't understand these stadium-security guys. Maybe it's leftover resentment from my kid-with-a-glove days, but I fail to see what purpose they serve. They're excellent at chasing away autograph-seeking kids but utterly useless when something truly bad goes down.

Under the ballpark, the maze of tunnels can be confusing to outsiders, because the walls all look the same, and there are never any windows. It's hard to maintain your bearings. If you weren't reading the signs on the doors, you'd have no way to know if you were two, three, or ten levels underground. Rookies sometimes get lost—it's a rite of passage—but at this point I've wandered through so many parks that I have a sixth sense about where things ought to be. You could turn me loose in a brand-new major-league stadium, someplace I'd never been, and I would find the trainers' room in fifteen minutes, blindfolded. Like a lab rat.

Coors Field I know well. I'm already down on the clubhouse level when a cop pushes past me at the fork where you go right for home and left for visitors. He fingers the radio hooked to his vest and barks a numerical code before taking off down the hall toward the Rockies' clubhouse. The equipment on his belt rattles in time with his strides.

"Officer!" I shout. And then, because you never know what will stop a cop in his tracks, I add, "I'm a player!"

The cop doesn't stop. I follow at a safe distance past the Rockies' weight room and the batting cage, past the room where they keep the portable X-ray machine. The walls down here are made of concrete blocks painted with a glossy off-white enamel to make them easier to wipe down. This part of the park can get dirty.

The cop stops just short of the locker room, joining a group of people—two more cops and some Rockies clubhouse personnel—in front of a door marked VIDEO.

I have almost reached the doorway when a man in street clothes stops me, palm to my chest. He's middle-aged, clean-shaven, with a square jaw and muscular shoulders. The silver in his close-cropped hair looks like it could have been applied with a brush, like he just stepped out of a Gillette commercial. His charcoal suit looks tailored and expensive. "This area is closed," he says in a deep, authoritative tone. "We'll send word to the clubhouses when you can come back."

It's nine-thirty in the morning. I'm wearing jeans and a hooded sweatshirt. How does he know I'm a player?

"What's going on here?" I ask.

"Nothing you need to concern yourself with."

"This is the Rockies' video room, right?" I step to the side, angling for a look.

The man cuts me off, grabs my shoulder, and pulls me back. "Listen," he says. "I'm not going to ask again."

Okay, now I'm pissed. I may not be the Best a Man Can Get, but I am a professional athlete. I reach out and grab the man's shoulders in both hands. With a quick torque, like a medicine-ball twist, I shove him against the wall. It's a hard throw, but, to my astonishment, he rebounds right off the concrete and comes back in a fury. He knocks out my feet in a swipe, then subdues me with a blow between the shoulder blades, all with military precision. Next thing I know, I'm pinned to the ground in a hammerlock, gasping for breath.

"Let the record show that I tried to persuade you, Mr. Adcock."

His voice is in my ear, hot and moist. And fragrant, like he gargles with cologne.

"You call that persuasion?"

He chuckles. "This works better."

I don't know who this guy is, but he knows who I am. I'll bet he's not eager to answer to the commissioner's office about the time he injured a player off the field in a completely preventable way.

"Let me go," I choke. "You're hurting my arm."

He loosens his grip and allows me to sit up. Behind him, the cop I had been following shuts the door of the video room. He squares up and crosses his arms over his chest like a sentry.

I stand and face the Gillette model. "That was a slick move, but you were too late. I saw everything."

"You didn't see jack. And let me tell you, it's lucky you didn't see anything, because a judge can pull you out of a game and put you on the witness stand in your uniform. The court doesn't give a damn what you do for a living."

I try another approach. "I was supposed to meet Erik Magnusson for coffee this morning."

"What time?"

"Half an hour ago."

"Well . . . your meeting got canceled."

Just then, two men hurry past us. Across the back of their navy-blue windbreakers is a single word in white block letters: CORONER. The cop at the door lets them in.

"What the hell?" The level of emotion in my voice surprises me. "Mags is dead?"

"I'm sorry." Gillette puts on his best community-policing face, tenting his eyebrows and frowning deeply. "It's a horrible loss. We'll brief the teams as soon as we have more information."

# 4

An hour later, I'm tying my shoes in the visitors' clubhouse, and you'd never know a man died two hundred feet down the hall. Players go about their sacred routines, washing and stretching and oiling their hair. Around eleven, when he can be sure everyone has arrived from the hotel, Bil Chapman gets up on a chair.

"Fellas, can I have your attention? Some of you remember Erik Magnusson, the Rockies' hitting coach, from his days as a Bay Dog. Well, I've got some hard news. Mags passed away this morning." I can see he's upset. Bil goes beyond the usual mother-hen mentality of the clubhouse manager. He gets seriously attached to his players. This modern era, when players switch clubs every couple of years, has been tough on him emotionally. Every twelve months, his family breaks up again. "I put a card for Magnusson's family in the trainers' room," he says. "I hope you'll find time to sign it."

Somebody asks what happened.

"We don't know yet," Bil says, "but it must have been his heart or something, right? I mean, the guy was in his early forties."

I think about the hints betrayed by the plainclothes detective. If Mags had died of natural causes, I'm not sure why he would have invoked judges, courts, and witness stands.

There's a buzz after Chapman steps down. The guys who knew Magnusson from his playing days gather in twos and threes. I avoid them until I join the line of guys waiting to sign the card. Two vets are talking with Thick Will Cunningham, our rookie first baseman. Thick Will is a man-child: six four, 240, and as dense as the hickory forest where he was born. As the nickname suggests, he is thick through the forearms, wrists, and other places where you can't fake it.

They're talking about Magnusson.

"It could have been a heart attack," says the first vet, a journeyman lefty starter named Grierson. "More likely it was a stroke."

"Absolutely," confirms the outfielder Lolo Quinn. "My money's on stroke."

"Why's that?" Will asks. With his buzz cut, braided belt, and Dockers, you could mistake the kid for a Presbyterian minister. A very large, very muscular minister.

The two older guys look at each other, then at Will. "You know Mags was a juicer, right?"

Will looks at his hands. It's strange, the way younger players handle talk of steroids. Guys my age will talk about it pretty freely, but the twenty-somethings, these kids who were in kindergarten the summer McGwire and Sosa were chasing Maris, they don't know how to react when someone brings up drugs. It's like they flash back to the DARE assemblies in middle school.

"I guess that explains it," Will says. He shakes his head slowly, as if to underline the shame.

"Every action has its consequences," Grierson says.

I suspected this was how the old-timers would react to Magnusson's death, and I'm furious. Even dead, he's presumed guilty.

"He was murdered," I interject. It's not what I meant to say—I was going to castigate the vets for spreading rumors—but now that it's out there, I can't help thinking it's true. Ruiz's guys threatened to kill Magnusson, and they did, end of story. It's Occam's razor: the simplest theory is usually correct.

Grierson laughs and shakes his head. "Only you would believe that, Adcock."

"You think it's possible?" Thick Will's blue eyes shine with curiosity.

Grierson sneers. "Why would anyone kill a hitting instructor? I mean, seriously, who would do that?" He scratches his name on the Hallmark without looking and hands the Sharpie to Quinn.

"A pitching coach, maybe?" Thick Will says.

"At least he'd log the bullets," Quinn cracks. "You're up, rook." He gives Thick Will the pen and slaps him on the ass. He and Grierson walk away, tittering.

"You might be right," Will says as he signs the card.

The Bay Dogs drafted Will out of high school as a pitching prospect, but in his first year of minor-league ball, he blew out his shoulder. Rather than let him go, the organization moved him to first base, where he performed well in the minors, showing flashes of power and solid glovework. He was called up to the big club for the first time last month, when our Opening Day first baseman broke his wrist. Everyone knows Will is on a short leash, because this year we're in the playoff mix, neck and neck with the Dodgers for first place in the National League West. At the moment, first base is one of our only weak spots. There are rumors of a trade-deadline move to bring in an established name. At any rate, Will knows he'll be moving back to

Fresno if he doesn't start hitting soon. Lucky for him, we're in Denver.

"So how are you feeling about your first trip to Coors?" I ask.

Will gives me the Sharpie and pulls an energy drink from his back pocket. In his enormous hands the eight-ounce can looks like a prop from a children's museum. "Clean air is good for the long ball," he says.

"It's the altitude, actually."

"You think so?"

"The air is thinner. The ball travels farther, because there's less resistance. It's physics."

"I got my fingers crossed."

"Just relax," I say.

Will exhales loudly. "I've been trying, man. Skipper says I'm pressing."

"Well, keep at it. Let the game come to you." I wince as the words leave my mouth. *Let the game come to you.* What can a kid do with that? All his life he's been told to be aggressive, to go out there and grab whatever he's after, and now people are telling him to relax? If I were Thick Will Cunningham, I'd tell me to fuck off.

Then I get an idea. "Have you heard of Tiff Tate?"

"The styling lady?"

"You should think about a consultation."

Baseball players are notoriously superstitious creatures. They'll wear the same pair of socks for weeks at a time if they're on a hot streak. The converse is also true: a slumping ballplayer will change anything if he thinks it might break the bad luck. That's why players sometimes alter their batting stance mid-season, or stop eating meat, or start a radical new weightlifting regimen despite the risk of injury. This urge is Tiff Tate's bread and butter.

"Isn't she expensive?" I can see him doing the math in his head. As a rookie, he earns a salary set by the players' union at less than half a million. Tiff's fee would be a significant chunk of his take-home pay. Of course, if it keeps him in the majors, it's worth it. Minor-league pay amounts to less than minimum wage, and remember that Will never went to college. If he fails out of baseball, his career options in rural North Carolina range from Jiffy Lube to his uncle's roofing crew.

I give Tiff's card to Will. "Just think about it. Sometimes it helps to know you have options."

He twiddles the card between his thumb and forefinger. "All right, man. I'll think it over." He slips the card in his back pocket and disappears into the weight room.

There: ten minutes went by and I didn't think about Magnusson's death. If the goal was to rattle me, then chalk one up for the bad guys: I'm rattled. I just took the case yesterday, and already there's a body. My hands shake as I sign my name on the card. I want to write something meaningful to his kids, something besides the usual condolences, but I know that doing so would only make me more conspicuous to whoever did this to him. Magnusson knew he was being watched. Chances are I'm being watched now, too.

Sometimes baseball is work, sometimes it's a bore, and sometimes it's a welcome distraction from life. At the most basic level, a ballgame is three hours when I can't do anything but sit and think (and sometimes play). Today I'm grateful for the time. I need to think.

On my way to the dugout tunnel, I pass a group of Bay Dogs coaches. Most coaches are former players, and as I've gotten older, their ranks have begun to include guys I played with. I saw this coming, and I thought it was going to be a harrowing experience, a constant reminder of the shadow of death. Turns out it's good to have dinner with guys my own age, who can relate to having a teenage daughter, to having a marriage fall apart. Kids like Thick Will Cunningham, bless his heart, haven't lived through any of that yet. I hate to admit it, but some of my closest friends are coaches.

As I try to squeeze past them, a guy I often dine with on the road, the third-base coach, Pete Lopez, reaches out and taps my shoulder. "There's somebody I want you to meet," he says. Pete pulls me into the group, and right away I'm confronted with the familiar face (and familiar charcoal suit) of the detective from the video room.

Mr. Gillette Model puts out his hand. "Johnny Adcock? Glad to meet you. I'm Jim Feldspar."

His handshake is strong verging on injurious. Were I right-handed, I would have been pissed. I try to remember that this is about him, not me, that this guy has a colossal chip on his well-muscled shoulder.

"We met earlier," I say.

Pete Lopez claps Feldspar on the back. "I could tell some tales about this guy. Jimmy and I roomed together in rookie ball. When was that?"

"Nineteen eighty-eight," Feldspar says. "Sarasota, Gulf Coast League."

"No kidding!" Billy Hacker is the bench coach, second in command to the manager. "I was with Clearwater in '88. How come we never met?"

The men all laugh and look down at their shoes, toeing the rubber floor of the locker room like it's dirt on the infield. This back-and-forth about the whens and wheres of your career may seem like useless reminiscing, but it serves a purpose. Coaching appointments are made by the manager without any kind of formal screening process. If one of these guys scores a manage-rial position somewhere, he'll have to fill out his coaching staff based on what and whom he remembers. There are no Craigslist postings for third-base coaches, no résumés or cover letters. These chitchats are all of that rolled into one.

"Listen, Adcock," Feldspar says, "I'm glad Petey caught you. Do you have a minute?" He holds open the door to the manager's office—currently empty, since Skipper is topside, pitching his daily half-hour of batting practice.

"Sure," I say. What choice do I have? When the commissioner's goon wants a word, you listen. Not that I'm expecting any surprises. I have a pretty good idea what he wants to say.

We part ways with the coaches and take seats in the office. As in all visitors' clubhouses, the manager's office is small and bare. An ancient Steelcase desk divides the room in half, with a rolling chair behind it and two metal folding chairs in front. Feldspar installs himself behind the desk like a big man. "How's the season been treating you so far?"

"No complaints. Team's in the race, and I haven't gotten killed yet."

"About that"—he purses his lips—"I'm sorry about Erik Magnusson. I came as soon as I could. It's terrible what happened."

I'm not sure how to react. He was there at the crime scene. Is he practicing his lines for reporters?

But if he wants to dance, I'll dance. "It's a shame," I say. "He was too young."

Feldspar looks me dead in the eye. "How about we be honest with each other?"

"Fine with me."

"What's your connection to Magnusson?"

"We were friends. Played together, kept in touch, that sort of thing."

"Be honest, Adcock."

"Does it surprise you that someone would want to be my friend?"

He starts to say something, then pauses. "This can't go on," he says.

"Excuse me?"

"I don't want to get technical—nobody wants the union to get involved—but the commissioner is aware of your hobby. He's taking it as a wake-up call, a cry of desperation from the players, and that's why I'm here. I have you to thank for my job."

"You're welcome."

"Thing is, now that I'm here, I'm supposed to do the detective work, not you. You're paid to throw strikes. No one wants you risking your life with extracurricular activities." He drums his fingers on the steel desk. "Like I said, I don't want to get into specifics, but the union contract prohibits side businesses, especially risky ones like yours."

"I could be wrong," I say, "but my understanding is that it's only a business if I get paid, and I've never taken a dime. What I do on my own time for my own enjoyment is not covered by the union contract. I don't see why it concerns the commissioner's office at all. I'm happy you're here, because with your connections I'm sure you can fix a million problems I can't, but you have to understand that you're essentially a cop, and plenty of guys are never going to trust a cop, especially with sensitive stuff."

"Sensitive like what?"

"I think you know."

Feldspar smiles and shakes his head, as if to say, "You mean pussy? Because I know all about that." But he doesn't, of course. Not the way a major-leaguer does. It's a blessing and a curse, the smorgasbord of women who throw themselves at you. They have a hundred names: Gamer Babes, Number One Fans, Hospitality Committee. If you're single—or if you're married but they know you fool around—they will find their way to you. They know the bus drivers and the concierges at the team hotel. They know the security guys who are supposed to guard the clubhouse. I've been propositioned in a bullpen restroom (no idea how she got in there) by a brunette wearing nothing but an unbuttoned Bay Dogs jersey. They're all free, all the time, no questions asked. It's not something you can explain to your friends back home, not without coming across like a jerk. You certainly can't tell your family. Only another player understands. Another major-leaguer—not a cop who topped out in rookie ball when you were in elementary school.

"How about this?" he says. "How about you continue to dispense your wisdom but cool the rest of it? No gunfights, no car chases, nothing that could land you on the DL or in jail or both. How does that sound?"

We both know this is only his first appeal. He has already mentioned the union twice, and not by accident. Over the years, I've helped quite a few of the players now serving as union reps, including Albert Echevarria, the current union president. Two years ago, during the off season, Echevarria was at a resort in Cancún when his teenage daughter disappeared. He suspected she'd been kidnapped, but he didn't go to the cops because (a) it was Mexico, and the cops were probably involved, and (b) his traveling companion, a woman, was not his wife. I made some calls from the comfort of my apartment in California, and we found the daughter two hours later, safe and sound in a wing of the hotel that was undergoing renovation. She wandered in and got locked inside . . . with a local surfer. So Albert owes me a favor, but I shouldn't kid myself. If the commissioner's office wants to make players' side businesses a sticking point in the next contract negotiation, my history with Echevarria won't mean shit. When players' paychecks are hanging on my cooperation, you can guess whose side the union will be on.

"Look," Feldspar says, "we're only talking about a year or two, right?"

"What do you mean by that?" I know what he means, of course, but I want him to say it.

He smiles. "Come on . . . you're not getting any younger. You can't pitch forever."

"Watch me," I say. "I'll pitch till I'm fifty. I'll be the zombie Tommy John, and you'll still be swapping Single-A stories with a bunch of coaches."

On that note I walk out, and for a few minutes I wonder if I went too far. But as soon as I emerge from the tunnel, hear the crack of the bat, and feel the grass under my feet, I realize I was right. This is my life. I may not be Clayton Kershaw, but I am immortal.

# 5

They play a lot of day games at Coors Field, more than any-where but Wrigley. In Chicago, the reason is tradition: Wrigley Field didn't even have lights until the early 1990s, and by that time Chicago fans were accustomed to the Cubs' playing their home schedule under the sun. The Rockies didn't exist until 1993. The Colorado preference for day games is an attempt to create the best possible playing conditions in a place where nighttime temperatures in April can dip below freezing. Even the night games start a little early. Everywhere else, night games start at 7:10 p.m., 7:15 p.m., 7:30 p.m. In Denver, they start at 6:40 p.m., God knows why. Today's start is 1:10 p.m., which means players report for work in the nine o'clock hour. I mention this not as a play for sympathy, but only to note that sometimes—not often, but sometimes—baseball players work nine to five.

In the eighth inning, the score is tied, with no outs and run-ners at the corners. Our starter, the righty Tim Wheeler, has turned in the Coors Field equivalent of a no-hitter: four runs on eight hits, six strikeouts, and no walks. He doesn't want to come out of the game—pitchers never do—but Skipper knows that games slip away fast in this park. Wheeler takes off his glove and grips it with his pitching hand. As he walks back to the dugout, he raises his ungloved hand, plugs a nostril, and shoots a snot rocket into the infield grass. Both runners are his, meaning they will be charged to his earned-run total if they score. If the Rockies take the lead here and end up winning, he'll be charged with the loss. The new statisticians like to say that a pitcher's record doesn't matter. That may be true for wins and no-decisions, but let me say this to the nerds out there: a loss is a loss. An "L" next to your name means you blew it, for yourself and the team. Nothing matters more than that.

The batter is Maurice Watson, the Rockies' callipygian third baseman, who is going to make his first All-Star team this year. Most observers credit Watson's success at the plate this season to the protection he gets hitting before Yonel Ruiz, but I always thought Watson had it in him to hit this well. He has a rare intensity at the plate, a reptilian fight-or-flight response that only a few players possess. You can't teach that. You also can't control it. Watson bats right-handed, so Skipper calls in a righty, Guillermo Gutierrez, to face him. The stars align for Gutierrez, and he gets Watson on three pitches—a sinking slider called a strike; a fastball at the belt, fouled back; and finally a piece-of-shit slider in the dirt that Watson can't resist but can't reach. It's tough luck. Even All-Stars make outs 60 percent of the time.

The visitors' bullpen at Coors Field is beyond the wall in right-center, next to a little landscaped area filled with pine trees and waterfalls that is supposed to represent the natural splendor of the Rocky Mountains. I think it looks like a Christmas-tree farm. As soon as Watson takes his final cut, I head for the gate near the trees. I don't even need to see Skipper's signal. This is my spot. This is why the Bay Dogs pay me. When a dangerous lefty comes to the plate in the late innings, it's my job to sit him down. It's my only job, in fact. I work ten minutes a night.

Why me? Dogma maintains that left-handed batters fare

worse against left-handed pitchers (and righties against righties), because breaking balls trail away from the hitter. Statistical analysis bears this out, but I tend to think the advantage is psychological. Imagine you're a hitter. It's late in the game, with runners on base, and just as you're walking up to the plate, the game stops so the other team can bring in a new pitcher, a specialist whose strengths match your weaknesses like hands on a mirror. Imagine further that this pitcher's only task for the night is to send you back to the dugout. After you, he can hit the showers, crack a beer, whatever. But first you. He's all about you. Every ounce of his professional-athlete's body is focused on this moment. For a hitter who might have four or five or even six at-bats that night, it's hard to match that intensity. Advantage pitcher, right?

Not always. The late-innings reliever has special concerns of his own. For one thing, the situation he inherits is always a shitshow—otherwise, he wouldn't have been called in. Today, for example, I'm coming into a tie game with runners on first and third. There's only one out, which means a sacrifice fly will score a run, as will several kinds of ground balls, depending where they're hit. So it's not enough just to get this batter out; I have to get him out in one of a limited number of ways. Of course, he could also get a hit, which happens on average two out of ten at-bats, no matter who's pitching or hitting. Bear in mind that we're in an opponent's ballpark in the eighth inning, meaning the crowd is liquored up and yelling at the top of their lungs. Also remember we're at Coors Field, a mile above sea level, so forget what I said about sacrifice flies: here, those are called "three-run homers."

I jog in from the pen, crossing paths with our second baseman, who is being replaced at the same time. This is what's known as a double switch, a maneuver that allows a manager to change two players at once and swap their places in the batting order. The pitcher's spot was up in our half of the ninth; now the new second baseman will hit instead. In the National League, where pitchers are required to bat for themselves, double switches are common, especially in the late innings of close games. Relief pitchers almost never bat, and when we do, our performance is laughable. The last time I stood on first base was six years ago.

The huddle on the mound consists of Skipper, Thick Will, and Tony Modigliani, our All-Star catcher. Modigliani is a prick, but he's our prick. It makes me feel a little better to know that he's due to bat in the top of the ninth. Even if I screw up and let the Rockies go ahead, I can count on Diggy to give the Rockies' pitcher the same heartburn Yonel Ruiz is giving me right now.

"All yours," Skipper says as he hands me the ball.

"Are you sure about this?" I shoot back. The joke isn't funny, and it never was, but now it's part of my routine. Skipper pats my ass and walks back to the dugout—leaving me, Thick Will, and Modigliani on the mound. "Head in the game," Diggy says to me. "We're looking for a double play. Low on the corners, got it?"

"Low on the corners," I repeat.

"No off-speed shit. Just the heater and the slider. No cutters, understand?"

"You're speaking English, Tony. I hear you." When I was traded to San Diego last year (it was a round-trip; I returned as a free agent at the end of the season), I had the pleasure of facing Modigliani twice. First time, I struck him out swinging. That was the highlight of my year. Maybe of my life. Second time, he spun around on a 2-2 fastball and put it twenty rows into the bleachers. Like I said, it's better if he's your prick.

The huddle breaks up and I take my eight warm-up pitches, including a couple of off-speed pitches and a cutter for Diggy's enjoyment. But when Ruiz steps into the box, I stop messing around. As much as I hate to admit it, Diggy is right: we need our heads in this game, or it's going south faster than a goose on crystal meth. These are the moments that decide championships. A win in June counts as much as one in September. In fact, if you want the games in September to count for anything at all, you have to win the ones in June. Sounds obvious, but when you're playing these games every day for six months, you have to be reminded. Diggy is just doing his job, the bastard.

Ruiz stands in the box like a locust on a branch, his massive arms furled and heaving with each breath. I try to see him as Tiff Tate does: the impeccable micro-beard like a dagger from lower lip to chin tip; the top two buttons of his shirt undone; the long, cuffless uniform pants, loose enough to hide the fullback thighs. From this mound I can't see details of his tattoos, but something is crawling up his neck, some kind of animal dancing with his gold chain and crucifix. Waiting, he pumps the bat up and down like a piston. Although we've not yet faced each other, I'm sure he's been briefed on my repertoire. He knows roughly what to expect, but most hitters like to see a new pitcher for themselves before they start making guesses about pitch selection. That's why I'm not surprised when he lets my first pitch sail past without so much as a twitch. It's a fastball at the knees, just touching the outside corner for strike one. Ruiz steps back with his right foot, leaving the left planted in the box. He stares down the line, reading the signs from the third-base coach. He knows as well as anyone the expectations here: get the ball into the outfield, pretty much anywhere, and the team goes ahead by a run. Maybe you get lucky and the ball carries farther, but a sacrifice fly is the minimum.

I know he's thinking fly ball, but I also know he's a wild man. He plays with a certain audacity—you might even call it greed—that you seldom see in American-born players. For example, on a routine single he never just trots to first and takes his base. Instead, he hauls ass down the line every time and rounds the bag at full speed, like he's going to try for second. The first couple of times he actually did get to second—until outfielders around the league wised up and realized there are no routine plays with Ruiz. A couple of strong-armed right fielders actually cut him down before he could scramble back. You'd think that would have stopped Ruiz from taking this kind of risk, but so far it hasn't. He's leading the league in stolen bases and pickoffs—a fan's dream and a manager's nightmare. Considering Ruiz's way of thinking, then, what are the chances he's going to be content with a sacrifice fly? Pretty small, I'd say, and I use this knowledge to my advantage. I want him to overextend, to chase something out of the zone. He'll be trying to golf it into the second deck, but if the pitch is already on a trajectory toward the earth, maybe even brushing the dirt, I might get a grounder. A strikeout would be nice, too.

Diggy knows what I'm thinking. He calls for a slider and sets the target six inches off the plate. I check the runners and deliver exactly the pitch I want, one that starts flat and hard before breaking down at the last moment, out of the hitter's reach. Except that this is no ordinary hitter. This is Yonel Ruiz. His reach is extra-human. Somehow he gets the bat on the ball, and it skips along the grass toward short. The infield has been playing at double-play depth, a few steps closer to the batter, and the shortstop fields the ball cleanly, turns, and fires to second. The second baseman receives the throw, jumps up to avoid the spikes of the sliding runner, and throws across his body to first, beating Ruiz by half a step. The inning is over. The Rockies don't score.

As Ruiz retreats back to the dugout, I surprise myself with a twinge of sympathy. Everyone in the park knows what he went through to get here, but few if any know that the nightmare is still going on. I think about his family stuck in their house in Havana and wonder if the Venezuelans at least allowed him to move his parents to a nicer place. I know so little about Cuba. Are there nicer houses to be had? Does the communist government allow that kind of upward mobility?

I saunter down the dugout steps, receiving ass taps and high fives from my teammates. My day on the mound is done, but I've got plenty of work ahead of me. For one thing, I need to get less ignorant about Cuba if I'm going to make anything of this case.

# 6

Diggy smacks a dinger in the top of the ninth, and we hold on to win by one. After a shower and shave, I slip out of the stadium by the employees' gate and find myself in possession of the real prize of a nine-to-five day: an evening of freedom. Most guys prefer day games at home, where they can spend the evening with their families, but for me there's nothing better than a matinee on the road. For a few hours, I'm a regular guy on a business trip—with ninety-five dollars per-diem meal money, handed out in cash every afternoon. I don't get recognized much in San José, but on the road I'm practically anonymous. Let's hope that sticks. This morning's events have me looking over my shoulder more than usual. If I were more prudent—and let's face it, less horny—I wouldn't be walking around Denver right now, but as it stands, I'm on my way to the Denver Public Library, workplace of Constance O'Connell, my date for the evening.

To be fair, she's more than that. Connie and I were introduced several years ago, and since then she has been my girl in Denver, a sympathetic soul with an open heart and a warm bed, and last winter I asked her for more than the usual casual liaisons. I had always wanted to spend a winter in the mountains, learning to ski, so I called Connie, who helped me find a short-term rental in Denver. As it turned out, I barely used my apartment, and I never learned to ski. I spent my days at the gym and my nights at Connie's place. I have never felt so cozy, inside and out. For three months, I felt like a sheepdog curled up by the fire. I've been with lots of athletic women—for example my ex-wife, Ginny, a four-year Division I soccer All-American. Connie is different; she likes to take a nap after lunch on Saturdays. Whereas Ginny used to wake me up at three or four in the morning for sex, Connie hasn't seen 3:00 a.m. since college, where she did run track, but only, as she would tell you, for the social connections.

Last winter was fantastic, but I worry that Connie may have gotten the wrong idea. She has been counting down the days to this weekend—the Bay Dogs' first visit to Denver this season—as though it were a homecoming. She needs to know that this isn't my home, that I don't want to settle down. Perhaps I should have been more explicit about my expectations, but I've never led her to believe that I'm anything but what I am. I do enjoy her company, but I enjoy the company of other women, too.

Okay, time out. You've read between the lines—gentle personality, nothing like my All-American ex—you're probably thinking Connie O'Connell is a dog. Nothing could be further from the truth. Her freckled cheeks, bangs, and dark eyes make you think of your best friend's nerdy older sister, the senior whose plaid uniform skirt you lifted in your fantasies freshman year. Thanks to Pilates and gentle weekend jogs, her body remains toned but not hard. At thirty-one, she has the curves a woman ought to have: the breasts God gave her and the ass she's earned. Her skin smells like cream, her hair like pine. Her vibe is wholesome and a bit naughty, like skinny-dipping in a private lake.

She is a librarian, though. The Denver Public Library is in

the civic-center complex downtown, across the plaza from the state capitol. It was built around the same time as Coors Field and designed by the American architect Michael Graves. The highlight is the Western History Reading Room, an atrium containing a three-story oil derrick made of salvaged timbers. Connie's office is right off the atrium, a little glass cube, like a greenhouse, taking in the rays from the skylights over the derrick.

My little hothouse tomato meets me in the courtyard outside.

"Hey there, beautiful," She's wearing an asymmetrical knee-length dress and strappy heels; her legs are bare. Acknowledging the cool summer night, she's brought a shawl for her shoulders, which lends a touch of elegance to the ensemble. "Thanks for meeting me," I say.

She rises on her toes, takes my head in both hands, and kisses me softly on the mouth. "Where are you taking me?"

I'm ready to bag the dinner reservation and go straight to her place. Her work clothes do that to me, for some reason. But I'm a gentleman. I lend my arm, and we walk the few blocks to the restaurant, a Michelin-starred joint called Chez Roque. Like Michael Graves, the chef at Chez Roque has adapted the conventions of his art for the Mountain Time Zone, with entrées like duck with pine nuts, filleted brook trout, and bison frites. Rocky Mountain oysters, I'm happy to report, are not on the menu. The hostess gives us a table by the window.

"How did it go this afternoon?" she asks. We haven't seen each other in more than two months. During that time we've talked and e-mailed, done a few video chats, but none of it compares to sitting right across the table, tracking her eyes with mine.

"We won."

She thinks about this. "When I was running track, I always thought it was more important to run a beautiful race than to win, because if someone else is faster you can run a flawless race and still lose, and then what do you have?"

"Nice thought," I say, "but it doesn't work in baseball."

"Why not?"

"Because baseball is a business, and winning is all that matters."

"Isn't that kind of mercenary?"

"It's completely mercenary. We're paid to win, not to play with grace and style."

Connie is the most principled person I've ever known. She once told me she likes filing tax returns, because it reminds her of our commonwealth. "But if it's a business," she says, "then you're selling tickets and beer and hot dogs and T-shirts and what else? Those foam hand thingies? Wouldn't you sell more of all of it if you looked good?"

"There's a woman you should meet," I say. "A stylist for baseball players."

"She helps them look better?"

"Yes, but her clients say that the real value is that they play better. She builds confidence."

Connie smiles. "Exactly."

"Exactly? You say the goal should be to play your best game. I say the goal is winning. How does Tiff Tate support your argument?"

"Because she makes your teammates feel good about what they're doing."

"You know what feels good? Winning."

"I'm not going to give up on this one, John. Winning isn't everything. If it were, then everyone would cheat."

"For a while, they did."

Her eyebrows drift up. Connie is not especially interested in baseball, but she likes the stories about men behaving badly.

I gear up to tell the story of the steroid era, where everyone is juicing, the authorities turn a blind eye, and corruption lurks behind every corner. But it doesn't feel right. Not today. Not with Erik Magnusson in the coroner's refrigerator.

"Put it this way," I say. "Wherever there is money to be made from games, you'll have players cheating. It's not just baseball. Think about insider trading."

"The stock market is not a game."

"If it's not a game, explain to me how a company like Uber, a company with no profits and a workforce of independent contractors, can be worth more than the rest of the transportation industry combined?"

"You know that's a complicated question." This is a long-running debate between us. Connie did her graduate internship at the University of Colorado's business library, so she knows a lot about this stuff. I know just enough to start arguments.

"The whole technology sector is bullshit!" I say. "Why is Tesla worth more than Ford?"

"Actually, it's not."

"Well, it's close. Too close, if you ask me. . . ." I pause. Out of the corner of my eye, I see something. Someone, rather. "Will you excuse me for a minute?"

I walk briskly to a table in the back of the restaurant, where a well-dressed Latino couple sit with their heads down, reading the menu. "Yonel?"

Ruiz's head snaps up. His eyes are inky black, the pupils nearly indistinguishable from the irises. The tattoo on his neck, I see now, is a dragon.

"It's Johnny Adcock, from the Bay Dogs."

I expect him to react one of two ways: either he'll smile and put out his hand like we're old buddies—this is the way of the ballplayer fraternity, especially in front of nonplayers like his date—or he'll pretend to be upset about the afternoon's game, ribbing me for throwing him junk, something like that. All in good fun, of course, even though I'm sure the loss stings.

Instead, he does something I could not have anticipated. He shakes his head and says nervously, *"No inglés . . ."* He shakes my hand weakly, with a sweaty palm.

*"Fine,"* I say in Spanish. *"I just wanted to introduce myself. Congratulations on an excellent season."* They are kind words, the type of encouragement I would have welcomed from a veteran when I was his age. But Ruiz does not thank me. In silence he flips his menu shut, looks at his watch, and then stares at the floor.

I turn to his date. *"My name is Johnny. I'm a ballplayer, too."*

*"Glad to meet you. I am Enriqueta."* She grips my hand in both of hers and squeezes.

*"My sister,"* Ruiz explains.

His sister? *"We are happy to have Yonel in our league,"* I say. *"Your brother is a very talented player, as I'm sure you know."*

*"It has always been a pleasure to meet my brother's friends, especially the ballplayers. . . ."* She laughs flirtatiously, but with an edge, as though there is more she might say on that subject if she felt I could handle it. Her eyes, I notice, are like the pitcher Max Scherzer's—heterochromatic, one brown and one blue. Heterochromatic eyes are usually the result of an injury in childhood or a virus that stopped the normal pigmentation in one iris but not the other. A lot of guys are envious of Scherzer's fastball, but I've always wanted his eyes. I imagine that crazy-wolf stare would be frightening on the mound. Anything that unbalances the hitter, no matter how small, can be worth dozens of outs over the course of a season. Even the tiniest hint of panic can be the difference between a smash and a soft ground ball.

"Your Spanish is very good, Señor Johnny. Have you spent time in Latin America?"

"Does Los Angeles count?"

She laughs. "You're funny. Join us for dinner?"

"Thanks for the invitation, but I can't."

"A drink?" Enriqueta reaches out and grasps my left biceps. "Surely you can stay for a drink."

"My date is waiting. Otherwise, I would." I turn to Ruiz. "Let's talk at batting practice tomorrow."

He shrugs.

As I turn to leave, Enriqueta stands up and blocks my path with her thigh. Her metallic minidress barely clears her crotch. "We should have dinner," she says. "If not tonight, another time."

"We'll see. I'm only in town for the weekend."

"You call me, we'll work something out. Middle of the night, it doesn't matter." She shakes my hand one more time, and when I pull back I find that she has slipped me a scrap of paper with her phone number written in purple ink. I am amazed. Does she keep these tucked in her bra?

Back at the table, Connie has ordered two glasses of white wine. "Who was that?" she asks.

"One of the Rockies," I say. "The new Cuban guy."

"Oh, Yonel Ruiz!" Connie cranes her neck to see. Ruiz's story has become so widely known that even a nonfan knows his name. Barely two months on the team, and already he's Peyton Manning.

"Yeah, I faced him this afternoon, but we've never met. I wanted to introduce myself."

"Did you get him out?"

"I did."

"So you wanted to gloat."

"Not at all. I didn't mention the game."

Connie eyes me suspiciously. "What did he say?"

"Nothing. He didn't want to talk."

"Well, he's entitled to his privacy. After what he's been through, on the motorboat and everything. The sharks. I can't imagine what it was like."

The waiter comes back and we order the bison. Connie starts to tell me about a crisis at work, something about an avaricious vendor of online journals. After a few minutes, I turn around to look in on Ruiz, but he's disappeared. The sister, too. The utensils are untouched, the table holding nothing but two sweating glasses of ice water.

# 7

Connie's apartment is in a former sewing-machine factory that a developer divided and converted to condos. A similar pad in San José would cost a million bucks, but this is not Silicon Valley, this is Denver, where a librarian can afford a decent life. The condo has all the touches you'd expect from a former industrial space: exposed brick, steel handrails, riveted beams. The concrete floors, however, are new. They contain radiant heating, which is an invention up there with toothbrushes, cars, and sliced bread. I have instructed my agent to look out for radiant-floor-heating companies in need of celebrity pitchmen. I don't even want to be paid; I just think the world needs to know.

After the wine (we had Saint-Émilion with the bison), we are both a little tipsy. Connie goes to the stereo and puts on some music, a band with guitars and two girl singers, whose voices swirl in and out of loose harmony. I can't remember the name of the band. I haven't listened to music with any intention— that is, actually putting on music, and thinking about my selections—since I was a teenager. Early in my professional career, I used to listen to whatever was playing in the team bus, but now that everyone's got headphones, I don't even hear that.

I feel like last winter Connie reintroduced me to an old friend. We cooked together, too: something else I used to do. Maybe it's Connie who's the old friend.

Her apartment is configured as a split-level loft, with the living and dining space below and the sleeping deck and toilet upstairs. I take Connie by the hand and pull her toward me. We kiss. Her mouth still tastes like the chocolate torte we had for dessert. She presses her body against mine, warm and soft.

"Let's go upstairs," she whispers in my ear.

Up we go. With a deft twist of the elbow, she unzips the back of her dress. Her shoulders slide out, and the garment collapses onto the floor. She's wearing lace panties and a bra made of fabric so sheer I can count the bumps around her nipples. Hardly what you'd expect a librarian to be wearing under her clothes, but you know what they say about judging a book by its cover.

I shake off my jeans and stretch out on the futon bed. For a moment she hovers over me on hands and knees, the ends of her hair tickling my arms. I want to get inside her as soon as possible, but I still haven't covered my agenda. I was going to do it in the restaurant, but then Ruiz got in the way. So I abstain a little more. "We need to talk," I say, pulling away just enough to look her in the eye.

Connie's lips are plump and shiny with saliva. "Later," she says.

"I'd feel better if we talked first."

She sits up. "I want to have this conversation, John. I do. But it feels . . . I don't know, manipulative? Unfair, at least. It doesn't feel right to be discussing commitment while we're having sex."

"We're not having sex yet."

She runs her fingers through her hair, shakes it back onto her shoulders, then unclips her bra and flops down onto the bed beside me. Lifting her pelvis, she slides out of her panties. Flight attendants have landing strips. Librarians, in my experience, prefer a three-volume set. "To be honest, right now I don't want to talk. Right now I want to make love."

Fair enough. She gets on hands and knees—her favorite—and puts that spectacular ass in the air. The girl singers tell us how lonely it can be in the great big metropolis. Connie and I do our part for togetherness. My grandfather once told me that you know a woman is the one when "as soon as you roll off her you can't wait to roll back on." I feel this way about Connie, but I remember feeling it for my ex-wife, too. (And plenty of women in between.) I suppose it's a cliché to say that the best orgasm of a man's life is the one he just had, but this one ranks in the top five for sure. My loins are still buzzing twenty minutes after Connie falls asleep.

That's at 11:00 p.m. By 3:00 a.m., my mind is playing another movie. In my head I'm back at the restaurant, talking to Ruiz, and he keeps shaking his head. *"No inglés . . . Mi hermana . . ."* I believe the *no inglés* part. English is the language of the imperialist pigs, right? In Cuba, they probably teach Russian or Chinese as a second language. But *mi hermana*? That part I don't buy. My suspicion could amount to naught, but Ruiz's silence is unsettling. It would have been unsettling even if Erik Magnusson were still alive. I have tremendous respect for Yonel Ruiz. To a large degree, I agree with Connie that his ordeal grants him permission to act however he likes. But it wasn't shell shock I saw tonight. It was something else; I'm not sure what.

*Tu hermana? Ay, amigo, I don't think so.*

By four-thirty, I've given up on sleeping. Very quietly, I gather my clothes and tiptoe downstairs to put them on without waking Connie. I write a note and leave it on the kitchen table: *Tonight we talk—promise!*

In the elevator, I dig in my pocket and find the slip of paper tangled up with the receipt from dinner. It's a New York City mobile number. I wonder how long Enriqueta is in town.

*Middle of the night,* she said, *it doesn't matter.*

I take out my phone. Anything for a case.

# 8

She's staying at the Ritz-Carlton downtown, midway between Connie's place and the team hotel. At first I'm puzzled why she's not staying with her brother, but then I remember my first big-league rental, a furnished month-to-month efficiency where I used an empty pizza box as a lap desk, not for convenience but because it was the cleanest surface in the apartment. Good times, but no place to put up your sister.

Under ordinary circumstances I'd walk, but, given the likelihood that I'm being watched, I call an Uber, apologizing to the app for trashing it at dinner. On my phone I watch the car approach, block by block, until finally it pulls around the corner. My fourteen-year-old daughter told me the other day about something called the Singularity, a hypothetical moment in which our real and virtual selves merge into a single consciousness online. I feel like I'm looking at it right now, but I could be missing something.

Enriqueta opens the door in a white silk chemise and matching thong. I never really doubted what she had in mind when she asked me to call, but this outfit pretty much settles the issue. Her thick, kinky hair is down, tumbling onto her shoulders and everywhere else. I realize that the tight little bun she sported at dinner was probably a victory, a feat of control. The hair has now returned to its natural state. Her breasts are also at liberty, swaying under the silk like chubby backup singers.

I slip into the dark room, and she leads me directly to bed. I'm not familiar with her perfume, a kind of woody frankincense that says as well as any words could that this is a woman—not a girl, but a woman, full stop. She falls out of the chemise, and I'm not sure what happens to the thong. Within a minute we're both completely naked. The riot on her head turns out to be the only hair on her body; the rest of her is so smooth it's almost slippery. Our limbs slide past one another as we wrestle—and it does feel like wrestling, each of us struggling for a stronger angle, a firmer grasp, a better exposure. She breathes in my ear and gently bites at the cartilage, whispering taunts in Spanish. Then one of her arms is around my back, pulling me down on top of her. The other hand is between her legs, then mine, darting back and forth, lining up the shot.

For the second time tonight I reach the cusp and pause. I raise myself up so I can see her face. *"Tell me about your brother,"* I say. *"Was it hard for him, coming here?"*

*"Hard?"*

*"Does Yonel talk about the men who brought him over?"* I try to make these lines sound unrehearsed. This is important, because, as enjoyable as this chore may be, information was my true goal in coming here (scout's honor). I slide my hand between her legs. Her thighs clench and relax as my fingers slip inside. *"I've heard they're very expensive."*

*"Yonel has plenty of money."*

This is either a lie or a misapprehension. According to Tiff, Ruiz is living on a pittance. Maybe Enriqueta doesn't know the smugglers are taking his salary? Or maybe she does know, but to her Cuban sensibility Ruiz's allowance feels like a fortune? I read that the per capita income in Cuba is less than five hundred dollars a year.

Then again, she's staying at the Ritz-Carlton in a room that costs five hundred a night.

*"I've heard stories. Cuban players being blackmailed by their smugglers."* I had to look up the word for "blackmail" on my phone on the way over here. I hope I'm saying it correctly.

*"What could they do? Yonel is already here."*

*"They could threaten his family. . . ."*

*"Don't you think I would know if my family was being threatened?"* Enriqueta wriggles away from my hand. She rolls onto her side and throws a leg over my hip like she's going to swing up into the saddle.

*"I think you would,"* I say.

*"Shhh. . . ."*

*"Can you put me in touch with Yonel?"*

*"You talk too much, Adcock."* She flips me onto my back and rises onto her knees. Then she walks up my body until she's straddling my neck.

*"I'm just—"* One more nudge forward. Now she's sitting on my face. For a moment I'm confused about how to proceed. I've never had an interrogation interrupted this way. I can think of only one thing to do. Closing my eyes, I press my tongue inside.

*"Now I talk,"* says the voice above me. *"Yonel is with this woman Tiff Tate all the time. Do you know her?"*

I am throwing myself into the task at hand, lips and tongue and everything, and Enriqueta's bucking hips tell me the effort is appreciated. But now she stops and slides off. Apparently her question wasn't idle chatter. She wants an answer.

*"It's not what you think,"* I say. *"Tiff Tate is . . ."* I don't know the Spanish word for "stylist," or even "consultant," so I just say, *"She's the woman who picks his clothes."*

Enriqueta clicks her tongue in disapproval. *"I told Yonel, don't pay for sex. In America, you don't have to pay. He doesn't listen."*

I could explain the difference between a prostitute and a stylist, but, honestly, it's a fine distinction, and I'm not sure my Spanish is up to the task. Also, my balls are starting to ache and it's nearly six in the morning.

*"Come down and ride my horse,"* I say. Tonight is the first time in years I've spoken Spanish during sex, and I'm simultaneously impressed and repulsed by my ingenuity. Ask anyone, I sound nothing like this in English. *"I need a cowgirl. Are you my cowgirl?"*

*"You want a cowgirl?"* Enriqueta slips happily into the charade. *"Okay, horsey, show me your tricks. . . ."* She rolls on a condom, and the next five minutes are a blur. We're sitting up, and she's straddling me. Her face is six inches from mine, and I'm staring into these crazy mismatched eyes, panting like an animal. We reach a kind of rhythm, and then our strokes gather speed until I'm no longer sure if I'm in or out. Except for the most basic biology, it couldn't resemble any less the sensuous, loving sex I had with Connie a few hours before. Finally, we finish and fall back on the bed.

Is it the eyes? Does Max Scherzer's wife feel like this every night?

While I catch my breath, Enriqueta props herself up on her elbows. A little moonlight comes through the chenille curtain, making the sweat on her forehead shine. She looks like she's been in a fight, hair leaping off in all directions, lips abraded, makeup smeared. I wonder if our tango took a turn she wasn't expecting. But she appears unhurt. No harm, no foul—right?

Enriqueta exhales emphatically. She wipes her upper lip with one manicured thumb. Then she says, matter-of-factly, *"So— where can I find Tiff Tate?"*

# 9

After a stop at the team hotel for a change of clothes, I walk to
Coors Field. It's 7:30 a.m., and I am the first player to arrive.
I walk around the field for a while, gathering my thoughts. A
lone groundskeeper mows the outfield on a John Deere trac-
tor. The sun is rising over the grandstand, filling the prairie
sky. It's a great location, a lovely stadium. For a pitcher, it's
almost worth the pain. This time the pain is worse than ever,
and it has nothing to do with getting knocked around on the
field.

The pit stop with Ruiz's sister has me confused for several
reasons. One is what she said about her brother's money, that
he has plenty, enough not to care about paying the exorbitant
fees of smugglers. It's possible she doesn't know the details of
his finances. Hell, lots of athletes themselves don't know where
their money goes. What's harder to countenance is that she
doesn't know her family is being held at gunpoint. There are
only two explanations for that: either she's estranged from the
family, or she's lying. I'm leaning toward the latter.

Or maybe Tiff is lying. At any rate, why does Enriqueta want
to meet her so badly? I understand that she could be jealous in
a protective, older-sister sort of way, but she misunderstood the
relationship between Tiff and Ruiz. Tiff may be sleeping with

Ruiz, but I doubt she is after his money—at least, no more than her fee.

My phone buzzes with a text message from Tiff. Maybe her ears were burning?

*Just heard about Erik Magnusson. You were friends, no?*

I thumb back a quick reply: *We were teammates. Thanks for your condolences.* I suspect she's trying to tease an update out of me, but I'm not ready. I want to talk to Ruiz at BP first. *Gotta go,* I tap out. *I'm at the park. No phones allowed.*

I descend to the visitors' clubhouse and start racking weights. I like to work out early, before the rest of the team reports for duty, but that's not always possible. Today I'm alone, so I plug my phone into the stereo system and put on the band Connie played last night. I finally remembered the name: Lucius. The cover of the album is a psychedelic drawing of a woman licking an ice cream cone, but when you look closer, you see that the cone is shaped like a cock. I'm embarrassed to say that I noticed this only after I sent the album to my daughter. *Catchy tunez, Dad,* Izzy texted back. *Not sure about the cover tho :-(*

I do my Saturday routine—back and biceps, plus cardio. Mondays and Wednesdays are quads and core; Tuesdays and Thursdays, chest and lats; Fridays, glutes and shoulders. I rest on Sundays, like that other famous setup man. It used to be that players worked out hard in the off season and not much during the year, but the latest thinking among trainers is that year-round conditioning is the key to longevity. It's counterintuitive, but working out six days a week ensures you have something left to give at the end of the season. This hasn't been a change for me. I have always worked out during the season, mostly because I can't sleep and don't like to watch TV, but it's been a difficult transition for some players, because now the season never really ends.

After lifting, I take a shower and grab breakfast from the

catering table as the rest of the team is filtering in. Everybody is talking about Thick Will, and when he shows up at 9:45 a.m., I realize why: gone are the Dockers and the plaid dress shirt, and in their place is a black velour track suit with yellow stripes and a pair of vintage Nikes. His hair has been bleached and spiked, and he's got zirconium studs in both ears. He looks like Eminem—or a Russian gangster on vacation.

Chichi Ordoñez, who plays shortstop and still believes in hazing rookies, makes a loud wolf whistle. Thick Will pretends not to hear. He reaches his locker without breaking stride. As he unlaces his shoes, I slide in next to him.

"Something you want to tell me?" I ask cautiously.

"Best night of my life, Adcock. That woman is incredible."

"What woman?"

"Tiff Tate! You should see what she keeps in her plane."

"She has a plane?"

"Yeah. I called her yesterday after we talked, and she squeezed me in. I met her out at the airport. She has this little jet, just a couple seats up front and a huge closet in the back, plus a barber's chair, mirrors, the whole deal. Even a piercing gun." He touches his earlobes tentatively.

"You know you have to take those out for games."

Will nods. "She gave me a sheet with all the rules. I'm supposed to put alcohol on them, but if they close up, I can just jam the posts through." He unzips the track-suit jacket, revealing a tank top made of black mesh. "Want to see the best part?" Under the mesh, on the left side of his chest, is a tattoo of a heart, still slick with ointment. Inside the heart is the name *Dee Ann*.

"Is Dee Ann your girl?"

"My mom," he says proudly. "I texted her a photo but I haven't heard back."

"Tiff did the ink?"

"She does it all."

"I'm impressed, Will."

"Actually, it's The Fizz."

"Fizz?"

"*The* Fizz. That's my nickname. Like a soda, light and sweet. While the bleach was setting, she gave me this lecture about names. She said 'Thick Will' sounds heavy and slow. From now on I'm The Fizz, light as air and sweet as honey."

I know other players who have had the Tiff Tate treatment, but I've never seen a transformation so dramatic. To be honest, I'm a little upset with Tiff. She sold this poor kid everything on the menu. I can only imagine how much she charged. I'm sure Will would tell me if I asked, but this isn't the time. I'm skeptical that the makeover will have any impact on what really matters, but on the off chance it does, I don't want to ruin his good run before it starts.

I'm also worried about how the other guys will react. Baseball players aren't the most tolerant people on earth. Ordoñez's whistles are nothing. Guys can be vicious when they detect weakness. A couple years ago, it got around that a rookie infielder named Contreras called his girlfriend in Puerto Rico before and after every game. Ordoñez and a couple others got a prepaid cell phone from 7-Eleven and started calling Contreras, pretending to be thugs from a drug cartel. They demanded money, a hundred grand or something, way more than Contreras had in his bank account. "We're watching your girl's house," they told him. "We can see her through the window." When Contreras called his girlfriend, he would break down in tears, telling her to be safe, to close the blinds. He never told her why—I guess he didn't want to worry her—but Ordoñez let this go on for a week before telling Contreras that he'd been punked.

Batting practice goes a long way toward shutting up Will's

critics before they have a chance to speak. His first swing lands in the Christmas-tree farm in center field, maybe 425 feet away, a nice hit, but not that unusual. BP is a special environment. For one thing, the pitching is cake: a never-ending feed of weak fastballs served up by our sixty-five-year-old manager and other members of the coaching staff. There's a school of thought that batting practice is counterproductive, because it builds false confidence in hitters. I'm not sure that's true; few hitters would tell you that the ability to hit a seventy-five-mile-an-hour fastball is any reason to feel confident at the plate. In fact, they all fear becoming what is known as a "five o'clock hitter."

That said, an impressive BP session always turns heads. Some players know this and organize their schedules around it. Skipper likes to talk about how, when he was playing for the Yankees in the late seventies, Reggie Jackson used to reserve the last BP slot for himself. He knew that the later he took BP the more fans would be in the stadium to see him hit. That slot, 5:45 p.m. or whatever, became known as "Reggie Time." On days when Jackson couldn't make Reggie Time—if he had an injury that required extra time in the trainers' room, for instance—he would make a show of giving away the slot. It was a form of patronage for lesser-known players.

This morning, Will gives a performance that would have made Mr. October proud. After he's warmed up, he starts sending baseballs into the upper deck above right field. Will bats left-handed, which means most of his power is to right, his pull side. But today he uses the whole field. Seven or eight pitches in, he starts muscling balls the other way, to left. He has a couple of nice drives, gappers that would have gone for extra bases. Then a ball clears the bleachers, slamming into the giant video board looming above the seats, maybe 475 feet from the plate. Now everybody stops what they're doing. Will returns to his strong side and pulls the next ball hard down the first-base line, where Chichi Ordoñez is doing some stretches on the warning track. Will's drive misses Chichi by twenty feet, but Chichi must have heard something whistling through the air, because he collapses like a folding chair as the ball caroms off the wall.

After Will steps out of the cage, no one congratulates him—it's just batting practice, after all—but it does take everyone a few seconds to resume their activities. I smile. Maybe The Fizz Cunningham will be okay.

At any rate, score one for Tiff Tate.

# 10

When the Bay Dogs finish BP, I hang back with Pete Lopez to watch the Rockies hit.

"Gotta say," Lopez says to me, "I think you dodged a bullet with Yonel Ruiz last night."

"Why's that?"

He looks at me. "You threw him junk, and he still made contact. Imagine if you'd missed your location. If you'd been an inch closer to the plate, that would have been a double, not a double play. Two runs in."

I hate this kind of talk. Everyone hates this kind of talk, fans and players alike, yet we are unable to resist. It's just too rich, too tempting, to imagine a world where the mechanism of cause and effect is so efficient that tiny adjustments change the course of history. For instance, what if Kirk Gibson had injured only one leg, instead of two, in the 1988 NLCS against the Mets? How might that have changed his famous pinch-hit appearance at the end of Game 1 of the World Series? The way it happened, Eckersley ran the count full, then hung a slider that Gibson muscled over the right-field wall for a walk-off win. The fact that Gibson could barely make it around the bases pretty much iced the hearts of the Oakland players, and the Dodgers went on to win the Series, four games to one.

But what if Gibson had been a little healthier? Would he have waited on that slider? He might have made better contact on one of the pitches he fouled off. He might still have launched that shot, but he also might have grounded out.

"But, Petey," I say, "I didn't miss my location."

"I know you didn't, I'm just saying it could have been bad. I mean, for Christ's sake, look at that. . . ."

We both watch the spot behind the cage where Ruiz is getting ready. He has a bat yoked over his shoulders, the pose that Bo Jackson made famous, arms bulging like pythons let into the rabbit hutch. He twists left and right, opening his back. No expression on his face. No teammates within six feet. He exists in a cone of silence, a bubble of perfect concentration.

"I'm going to chat him up," I say to Lopez.

"Seriously?"

"Watch me."

I walk casually across the apron of green turf behind the plate, approaching Ruiz from behind. For some reason, I wish I had a prop, a bat or a glove to play with, something to absorb my nervous energy. When I'm four or five feet behind him, I hook my thumbs in my belt and just stand there for a minute, watching the batter in the cage. It's Dan Anglin, the aging first baseman whose swing was consuming Magnusson the night he died. Something is indeed wrong with his approach, that's pretty clear. Anglin fouls three pitches into the dirt, cursing under his breath. Ruiz stops stretching and watches. I wonder what he makes of Anglin's struggles. Hard to imagine he's too sympathetic.

"*What do you think?*" I say in Spanish. "*His timing is off, no?*"

Ruiz turns around slowly. He recognizes me but says nothing, and returns his attention to the cage.

"*I know you're being watched,*" I say. "*Tiff Tate asked me to help you.*"

Ruiz lowers his head and swings the bat gently back and forth like a golf club. His lats strain the sides of his pullover BP jersey. *"Go away,"* he says without turning around.

*"She explained the trouble you're in. I want to help. I need you to put me in touch with the smugglers. Do that, and the problem will go away."*

*"You don't know anything."*

*"Not yet. I need to reach the Venezuelans. Can you make that happen?"*

Ruiz turns his head to the side, careful not to make eye contact with me, but he wants me to see the grimace on his face. *"You want to help me, huh?"*

*"Yes. It's bullshit, what they're doing to you. We have to stop them."*

*"Were you helping me last night?"*

Does he know about me and his sister? Mea culpa . . . but, come on, this can't be the first time that has happened! Like she said, she loves ballplayers.

*"Yes, I was trying to help."*

He laughs. *"How about you help yourself and fuck off?"*

What's that? I'm out here risking my life for this bastard, and he tells me to fuck off? I've had unsatisfied clients before. Pretty much every guy who asks me to investigate his wife gets pissed off when I deliver the dirt. (Here's a tip, fellas: if you think she's cheating on you, she probably is. Don't act surprised.) But this is something else entirely. I'm trying to *save* his wife—and his daughter, and his parents, and his eight-figure contract. If he wants me to fuck off, he doesn't have to ask me twice. I'm done.

In front of the visitors' dugout, Pete Lopez stops me. "So how did it go? Friendly guy?"

"Not really," I say. "I prefer his sister."

# 11

The game is a rare Coors Field squeaker, with good defense supporting solid starting pitching on both sides. The score is tied 3–3 going into the eighth, when I get the call to warm up. Ruiz is due up third, but the two hitters before him are also lefties. I might be asked to pitch to any or all of them. Most likely Skipper will save me for Ruiz, because of my success against him yesterday. Lucky me.

As I limber up, tossing to the bullpen catcher from forty feet, then fifty, and finally from the rubber, I play through what's going to happen. They call this "visualization." Phil Sutcliffe, our pitching coach, took a seminar last winter and taught us the technique in spring training. "Make the warm-ups count," he says. "Pretend you're in the game already." All year I've been skeptical, and I've done the visualizations only reluctantly, but today I can use the help with my focus. I imagine Ruiz crowding the bullpen plate, his folded arms heaving on every breath. I start with a fastball low and away, barely clipping the outside corner. In my visualization, I get a called strike, so I make a note to go there again, but not right away. Then I switch sides, moving inside with a front-door slider. If thrown correctly, the front-door pitch looks inside until the last possible moment, when it jumps out over the plate. You know that kind of slider is working when the hitter pulls his hands back. In my visualization, he does. That's strike two. Now I imagine that it's 2-2—I'm still ahead in the count, with a ball to spare—so I try a slider in the dirt, outside. I'm hoping he'll chase, but in this visualization, he does not, so I return to the outside fastball that worked for strike one: on the black, at the knees. Strike three. I actually feel relief as I imagine the end of the at-bat, seeing Ruiz walk off the field, dejected, inning over, game still tied. He will have left a runner in scoring position against a thirty-six-year-old finesse pitcher who makes a fraction of his salary. Visualization is powerful stuff.

When the call comes, it's for Ruiz, just as I expected. I jog out to the mound and take my eight warm-up pitches. Then the plate umpire, Joe South, tosses me a new ball. I remove my glove, tuck it under my elbow, and take a walk on the grass next to the mound, rubbing up the fresh ball. I review the plan: fastball away, front-door slider, fastball away. It couldn't be any more straightforward, but I'm finding it difficult to concentrate on the task at hand. This is what visualization is supposed to help with—Sutcliffe calls it the "monkey mind." I'm thinking about Magnusson, about how the drink we shared the other night turned out to be his last. Then I'm thinking about Enriqueta, with her bucking pelvis and crazy eyes. Maybe Feldspar is right: maybe I should stop doing investigations. It's got to be a sign when your clients start telling you to fuck off.

I climb back up the mound, plant my left foot on the rubber. Ruiz strides purposefully toward the plate. When he steps into the box, our eyes meet. He has dark, beady eyes. Nothing like his sister's. I see the sheen of sweat on his nose, the clean line of his Tiff Tate beard. *You ungrateful bastard,* I think. *You don't deserve to be here.*

This transcends the monkey mind. This is the tiger mind, the white-shark mind. It's dangerous—not at all what you want your pitcher to be thinking in a high-leverage, late-innings situation. In the abstract, anger is fine. Even motivational. There are plenty of angry pitchers. But I should have used my anger to put another two or three miles per hour on the fastball. Instead, what I do is lean back, gather all my strength, and aim my first pitch—a ninety-mile-per-hour fastball—squarely at Ruiz's heart. He turns away, and the ball strikes his back with a sickening thud, like an axe on a chopping block. Ruiz collapses in the dirt. The umpire throws his hands up to call time, but you can't hear his voice over the boos from the crowd. Colorado's trainers and coaching staff rush toward the fallen man. The rest of the Rockies charge the mound, where they are met by the Bay Dogs, who have leapt off their bench. I throw down my glove, getting ready for battle, and then I feel someone grab my arms. It's Will Cunningham. He pulls me back into a sea of gray jerseys, away from the pin-striped mob. Everyone is yelling now, in English and Spanish, but nobody is as loud as Joe South, the plate umpire. His mask is off and he's scampering after me. "You!" South shouts. "You're gone, buddy!" He jerks his thumb dramatically, eliciting a roar from the crowd.

Skipper totters over and gets in South's face. "Why the hell are you ejecting him? It was an accident, for Christ's sake!"

"You call that an accident? He threw right at him!"

"Pitchers make mistakes, Joe."

"Sure they do, but that wasn't one of them."

"Who the hell are you to say if it was a mistake or not?"

"I'm the goddamn plate umpire. It's my job."

"Hell of a job you're doing . . . a bullshit job!"

"One more word, Terry, and you're in the clubhouse with your pitcher."

"How the hell do you know the ball didn't slip out of his hand? Can you read his mind?"

South jerks his thumb again, ejecting Skipper. Another cheer from the crowd.

Now that he knows he's gone, Skipper turns it up a notch. We call this "getting your money's worth." He calls South a jackass. South calls him senile. You'd never guess these guys are friends. Bass-fishing buddies, if you can believe it, with winter homes in Florida just a few miles apart. When Skip's wife passed a few years ago, he moved in with Joe and Sharon South for a month. My point is that, as angry as they are, this is basically theater. On the video board in left field—the same spot "The Fizz" Cunningham hit in batting practice earlier—these two old men, now twenty feet tall, vent their spleens belly to belly. I have to believe some part of them loves this.

"You're too old to be calling balls and strikes," Skip yells, his face getting redder by the second. "And if you can't even see the strike zone, how the hell can you tell if my pitcher meant to hit this guy? You can't see shit, Joe! You know what you ought to do? Retire! You ought to retire!"

"I ought to retire? Who's the one getting up to piss eight times a night?"

"At least I still have my prostate!"

Apparently, this is Skip's last insult. The tank is dry. He taps me on the ass. "Let's go." By this point Yonel Ruiz has shaken it off. He stands on first base, glowering.

I follow Skip into the dugout, where we pace for a minute while Skip gives the bench coach instructions about what to do in his absence. Then we walk down the tunnel to the clubhouse. In the manager's office, Skip grabs two cans of Diet Coke out of the fridge and throws one at me. He turns on the TV. In silence, we watch as our new pitcher, Malachy Garcia, gets the next batter to ground into a double play, ending the inning. The TV screen changes to a Rockies logo on a purple background.

"So," I say.

"What the hell happened out there, Adcock?"

"It's like you said—the ball slipped."

"Spare me the bullshit. I know you threw at him. Joe South knows it. You're lucky it hit his back and not his head. As it is, you may be facing suspension."

"Nah . . ."

"Off the record, you threw at him, right?" Skipper is putting me in a tough spot. Pitchers never admit to throwing at a batter, even when the batter deserves it, and that isn't just machismo: although it is sanctioned by the unwritten, Old Testament code of baseball ethics, intentionally throwing at a batter is forbidden by baseball's actual written rules, and if you admit to breaking those rules, the commissioner's office will have no choice but to fine you, and maybe more.

"What am I supposed to say, Skip?"

"If I were in the league office, I'd sit your ass down for a week." Skipper taps his forehead. "Something ain't right up here, that's what I'd be thinking. So let me ask you again— what the hell happened? Why'd you throw at that poor fool? Have you heard what he went through to get here? There were sharks circling his ass. Hungry sharks. Do you have any idea what that's like? I don't, and with luck I never will. And now you're trying to break his back with a fastball?"

"I didn't break his back, Skip."

"Is there something you want to tell me? Something from your other career?"

Like everyone in baseball, Skipper knows what I do in my spare time. He's never been bothered by it, but it's his job to make sure I know where my bread is buttered. His message is essentially the same as Feldspar's, but his manner is more collegial. He was a player himself way back when—a good player, a catcher, with a long big-league career. He knows every player has something that keeps him sane, some blowhole or release valve or mountain-retreat-of-the-mind. Some guys drink. I have this. He gets it. But he's right.

"I've got it under control," I say.

"I'd say you don't, given what I saw out there. I'd say you were about eighteen inches away from ruining a young man's life."

"Listen, Skip, it's a personal matter. . . ."

"I'll tell you what's personal—this goddamn team! This is my team. I don't give a shit what you do when the ballgame is over, but when you're out there on the mound, you're working for me. Do you understand, Adcock? For three hours every night, I own you. And when you fuck up—and, bullshit aside, that's what you did today—when that happens I get angry, because that's my ass on the line. My ass, not yours."

"I know, Skip."

"Do you? Only two kinds of people get wins next to their name: pitchers and managers. Which means you and me should be seeing eye to eye here. But we're not. Why is that, do you think?"

"I'm sorry, Skip."

"It's not time for you to apologize. I'm not done yet. Why is it that our interests aren't aligned? One possibility is that your ship has sailed."

"My ship?"

"You're too old. Know why you didn't break that bastard's back? Because you're throwing batting-practice fastballs. Don't argue, you know I'm right. Your velocity has been slipping. These days, your game is all location and switching speeds. But what happens when you can't hit your spots, or when your fastball is just as slow as your off-speed stuff? You're not far from that point, Adcock. You and I both know it. So I'm thinking maybe that's what's going on here. You're washed up, but you don't see it. Or you won't admit it."

"You want me to quit?"

"The other possibility is that this investigation thing has gotten out of control. I don't know what you want with Yonel Ruiz, but I do know that if he's connected to one of your detective hunts, this is the first time it's influenced a game. I'm a reasonable man, Johnny, but when it comes to wins and losses, I'm a goddamn psychopath. This is your first and last chance, understand? You can apologize now."

"I'm sorry, Skip."

He points to the office door, and I leave. Psychologists tell us that losing hurts more than winning feels good, and they're right. To hell with winning being the only thing—*not losing* is what really matters. Fear of losing, or, more accurately, hatred of losing, is the secret behind all great athletes, from Michael Jordan to Mike Trout. Because the accounting is the same, the distinction between winning and not-losing gets muddled, but there is a big difference. Ask any ballplayer, and he'll tell you the same thing: winning is good, but, man, *fuck* losing.

Ironically, the ability to shrug off a loss, to move on and compete the next day without the mental weight of yesterday's outcome, is essential for success at this level. It's especially true when you play every day, or nearly every day, like I do. Today I blew it, but tomorrow, if Skipper asks me to pitch, I need to walk onto the mound with a clean slate and a case of amnesia. This is what ballplayers mean when they say they're approaching their season one game at a time. Tomorrow you won't remember today. You just can't.

# 12

I shower alone and put on my street clothes. On the muted TVs suspended from the ceiling, I see that the score is still tied upstairs, going into the tenth. The silence in the empty clubhouse is profound; the only sound is the rumbling of the ice machine outside the trainers' room.

I have plans tonight with Connie, another romantic dinner followed by another cozy evening at home. Looking back on last night, I'm glad we didn't get to talk about commitment—and not just because I slept with another woman a few hours later. I'm not sure I've changed my mind on the subject, but suffice it to say that my feelings are evolving.

Behind the wired-glass window of the manager's office, I see Skipper with his feet up on the desk, shouting at the TV screen. He finishes his Diet Coke and throws the can at the wall. Skip was married forty-two years, but he behaved like this even before his wife died. Maybe marriage brought him comfort. He certainly never showed it.

Very quietly, I rise and walk through the trainers' room to the hall between the clubhouses. A few people from the Rockies' media-relations team are already hovering outside the room used for postgame interviews, thumbing at their phones. The video room is just around the corner. I take a peek and see that there's a security guard sitting on a folding chair in front of the door. I pat my pocket to make sure I have my ID on me. On the road, you can't depend on security guards to recognize you out of uniform. With a head-down, businesslike stride, I turn the corner and approach the door. A length of yellow police tape runs diagonally across the doorway like a pageant sash.

"Hey, can I get in there for a sec?" I ask the guard. "I left my notebook on the desk."

"Sorry, man. No entry tonight. If you need to watch tape, you can use the video suite in the executive offices upstairs."

He is in his mid-twenties, athletic build, goatee. Seems like a decent guy. Given another outcome in the genetic lottery, he could have been in the Bay Dogs bullpen instead of me. Instead, he's stuck on a folding chair in a windowless hallway.

"That's cool," I say. When trying to relate to members of the post-*Jackass* generation, I try to sound as young and casual as possible. In practical terms, that means imagining how my daughter would say things. "No worries. I just need to grab my notebook and I'll be outta there."

The young man looks at me. "Seriously? I just said no."

"All right, look. I'm on the Bay Dogs, I'm a pitcher, and I need—"

"Johnny Adcock. I know who you are."

"And what's your name?"

"Jeremy."

"Okay, Jeremy, what's it going to take for you to let me in there?"

Jeremy leans back. The top lip of the folding chair tinks against the wall. "You'll have to find me another job, for one thing, because I'll get fired. See the police tape? Somebody died in there."

"He was a friend of mine," I say. "Erik Magnusson."

"That sucks," the kid says. "But I can't let you in."

"What if I told you there was an old man having a heart attack in the visitors' clubhouse?"

"Is that true?"

"You'd better check, right? 'Cause, if he was having a heart attack, and your boss found out you knew about it and didn't check—I'm guessing you'd lose your job for that, too."

He thinks about this for a minute before realizing I've got him. He stands up. "You say it's an old man?"

"In the manager's office."

He jogs away, and I duck into the video room. It's a tiny, windowless cell with the same block walls as the hallway. Folding tables line the walls. Normally, you sit down in front of a laptop at one of these tables, but the laptops are gone and the tables are covered with a fine dusting of black fingerprinting powder. Above the center of the room, the acoustic ceiling tiles have been removed and an exposed steel beam has been marked with yellow spray paint. I look closely at the beam. Pink nylon fibers, like those from a cheap rope, are lodged in the steel's fireproof coating.

Was it a suicide? Based on what Mags told me at the bar about his family life, it sounds like he had plenty of reason to be depressed. But why wouldn't he just get a gun? In this state, they practically hand them out free at the airport. Hanging yourself is what you do if you're trying to make a statement with your death. Mags was a modest man. If he were going to kill himself, he'd do it in private. He'd just disappear and never come back, like an ailing cat.

A jug of mineral water sits in the cooler on the far wall, alongside a whiteboard with all the markers still lined up neatly in the aluminum tray. I kneel to look under the desks, but the cops have swept the place clean. Aside from the tables, the water, and the markers, everything not bolted down has been taken away by the evidence collectors. I am making one final pass across the center of the room when I hear something skitter across the square of exposed concrete. I bend down and search the perimeter of the carpet until I find it. At first I think it's a bit of chipped concrete, but then I see that it's hollow inside. It's a tooth, or part of a tooth. The hole inside is still pulpy, like it was only recently chipped.

I turn around to see if I've missed anything. The whiteboard is full of notes about struggling Rockies. At the top of the board is Dan Anglin, the first baseman who was giving Magnusson heartburn. Next to his name are some dates: *5/15, 4th PA; 6/22, 1st PA.* "PA" stands for "plate appearance," so these must be reminders to look at those particular at-bats. Maybe Mags saw something that could be corrected? Then I see a name that doesn't belong on the board: Yonel Ruiz. I can't imagine why Ruiz would be listed alongside Anglin—God knows, he doesn't need any help at the plate. Below Ruiz are two more strange inclusions: Fausto Carmona and Roberto Hernández. These guys are even more out of place than Ruiz because: (a) they play for the Astros, (b) they are pitchers, and (c) they are the same man.

The same man? It's an odd story. Fausto Carmona is the name of a Dominican pitcher who had a couple of excellent seasons with the Cleveland Indians before it was discovered that he had changed his identity, and his age, years ago. When the fraud was discovered, his visa was revoked and he was suspended by MLB. He appealed and eventually clawed his way back. He now pitches in the Houston Astros organization under his birth name, Roberto Hernández.

What was Magnusson trying to say here? I look more closely at the names and notice that they are laid out in a kind of two-by-two grid, with Carmona and Hernández directly below Ruiz and someone named Pascual Alcalá. I take a picture with my phone and leave the room.

The kid is back on his chair. "Old man was fine," he says. "Just angry."

"Thanks for checking."

"Just doing my job." He reaches up and pantomimes tipping an invisible cap.

Back in the clubhouse, I watch Skipper crack another Diet Coke. I wonder what the kid said to him: *Excuse me, sir? Are you okay? Are you having a heart attack?* I think we're lucky there wasn't another murder just now.

On the muted TVs hanging from the ceiling, the game heads into the bottom of the eleventh, score still tied. This could go on indefinitely. I'm under no obligation to stay, having been ejected from the game, and with the new information about Magnusson's death, I'd like to make some inquiries before I have to meet Connie. I'm not sure what to think about the tooth. If it was murder, the chipped tooth suggests that Mags fought back. But there were no signs of a struggle—no blood-stains, no scuff marks on the wall. Hell, the water cooler was still upright. Maybe the killer found Magnusson asleep, killed him with a blow to the head, and then strung him up to make it look like suicide. Makes sense, but it would be hard to prove without access to the body. And it doesn't explain the tooth.

The names on the whiteboard, though—I'm curious about that, and I have a source who may be able to shed some light on the situation. I reach up to disconnect my phone from the charger (I wasn't bullshitting Tiff when I texted her about phones at the park—they're prohibited during games by MLB rules). Then, all of a sudden, the damn thing rings, breaking the fune-real silence and scaring the shit out of me. My left hand shoots out so fast that I knock the phone off the shelf. It dangles on its cord like a terrier straining the leash. The screen reports a call from a blocked number. I tap the green button to answer.

"Johnny Adcock . . ." The voice is languid, robotic, and

indistinct, as though it has been run through a digital filter. I immediately think of the call Magnusson received in spring training, the one that warned him against talking about Ruiz.

"Who is this?"

"I have information you may find useful. You will receive a text message with an address. Be there at eight tonight."

"I'm not coming unless you tell me who this is." It's an empty threat, and the caller knows it. He hangs up without another word.

Suddenly I'm back in the empty locker room, listening to the pulse in my ears. Then I hear a rumble—that's the crowd in the stands several stories above me—and on the TV I see the Rockies huddled around the plate, bobbing up and down in anticipation. Yonel Ruiz trots down the line from third, his face conspicuously devoid of emotion, like he's too tough to feel joy, but then, at the last minute, he tosses his helmet in the air and enters the mêlée.

A moment later, I hear voices in the tunnel and the clicking of spikes on concrete. Although I am not technically responsible for the loss—Garcia got the double play after I hit Ruiz—my mistake no doubt shifted the momentum of the game. The box score is one thing, but if the beat writer is doing his job, the wrap-up will capture what the score can't—that San José's Johnny Adcock inexplicably threw at Yonel Ruiz in the bottom of the eighth inning, lighting a fire under the Cuban slugger, who hit a walkoff homer in the eleventh.

*Fuck losing.*

The phone vibrates in my hand as the text arrives. It's a Denver address, West Forty-fourth Avenue. I have no idea where that is, but, lucky for me, the geniuses who designed my phone are one step ahead. I click the address, underlined in blue, and a map appears. After some stretching and scrolling, I see that it's in an industrial zone five miles north of the ballpark. The phone even shows me a photo of the building, which looks like a printer or an auto-body shop. With a few swipes I've walked around the block, checking out half a dozen identical warehouses. I've never been there, but I can predict with confidence that this neighborhood will be deserted at 8:00 p.m.

Here's the thing about me: it's not that I can't tell the difference between a good choice and a bad one, it's more like good and bad aren't what I consider when I'm planning my life. Remember when I said I was done with Ruiz? And remember how all I wanted tonight was to hide out in Connie's loft? Those were good, safe choices. But safe choices don't inspire me. A phone call from a disguised voice, asking to meet in an industrial zone after dark? That's your classic bad choice. And yet, as soon as I receive that call, I know it's what I'm doing tonight.

Sorry, safety. Sorry, Connie.

I hit a batter today—and now this?

I'm a bad man.

# 13

I leave the ballpark at five, after telling every reporter who asks what I told Skipper a few hours before: It was an accident. The ball slipped. If you repeat a line often enough, you start to believe it yourself. I walk out of there feeling wrongfully accused.

The case is heating up. I want to check in with Tiff before this meeting tonight. I've found that if you don't update your clients regularly—even if you have nothing major to report—they start arriving at their own conclusions, and that can be disastrous. When I first started doing matrimonial cases, I had a client, a teammate, who hadn't heard from me in a week, so he decided to take matters into his own hands. He sneaked into the house and kidnapped his own children while his wife was taking a nap. As you'd expect, she freaked out and called the cops, who tracked him down at a nearby motel and led him away in cuffs. So, yeah—update your clients. Just do it.

I dial Tiff, and she answers on the first ring.

"I spoke with Ruiz this morning," I tell her.

"Not over the phone," she says. "Come to the airport. I'm at General Aviation."

I'm surprised that she's in Denver, until I remember what she did to Thick Will.

"Great. I'll get an Uber."

"No need. I'll send my driver."

"You have a driver in Denver?"

Tiff laughs. "I have a man in every port. Does that shock you? Are you scandalized?"

"A little," I admit. "I realize it's a double standard."

She tells me a hostess in the GA terminal will escort me out to the plane. "Ask for John Rockenbush," she says.

"Who's Rockenbush?"

"Nobody. It's just a name I use."

Just a name? I'm sorry, but "John Rockenbush" is just a name like "Doug Fister" is just a name. And "Antonio Bastardo." And "Brad Peacock." You'd think if she was looking for cover she would have chosen something more pedestrian, like "Tom Smith." But this is Tiff Tate we're talking about. I'm quickly learning that character is everything to her.

Speaking of names, I'm eager to start digging on Pascual Alcalá. While I'm waiting for Tiff's car to show up, I call Anibal Martín, the Bay Dogs' Cuban scout. Don Anibal was a big star on the Cuban national team in the heady days after the revolution, and his name still carries weight in certain circles. He's tight with the officials in the visa office, and he has been helpful on more than one occasion having nothing to do with scouting talent. The phone rings intermittently for nearly a minute—love those communist phone lines—before he answers.

*"Vale!"* he grunts. I picture him sitting with his feet up on a scarred wooden desk, a fat stogie dangling from his tobacco-stained lip. Maybe there's a girl in the kneehole? He's an ugly old bastard, but you never know.

*"This is Johnny Adcock,"* I say in Spanish. *"Is this Don Anibal?"*

*"Fucking Adcock! How the fuck are you, little cunt?"*

We've met in person only once. Martín talks to everyone like this, one reason the organization has never offered him a State-side job. I've always found him delightful—a throwback to the days when front-office personnel were a little less impressed with their own importance—but I have a weakness for Spanish profanities.

*"Not bad, my friend. You?"*

*"Same shit. Maybe a little worse, because I'm getting old. For the last six months, my rod won't stand up straight. It curves to the side like a shepherd's crook. That ever happen to you? No—you're far too young!"*

*"I'm not so young anymore, Don Anibal."*

*"Not like me, coño. You'll see, one day!"*

We share a laugh. Martín coughs, hacks up some phlegm, then comes back. *"So what's on your mind, turkeydick?"*

*"I have a favor to ask. Have you ever heard of a player named Pascual Alcalá?"*

*"Alcalá? Maybe. What's the first name again?"*

*"Pascual."*

*"An Easter baby, huh? I don't know the name, but I'll check it out. Give me a couple days?"*

*"That would be great, thanks."*

I give him some gossip about the front office in San José, and he reciprocates with a detailed anatomical description of Raúl Castro's new twenty-six-year-old mistress, a former volleyball star who evidently makes Sofía Vergara look like Bea Arthur. Before we hang up, I instruct him to write down my cell number and read it back twice.

I have one more call to make. This one I've been dreading. I feel bad for breaking tonight's date with Connie, but I've decided it's better than just standing her up.

"Listen," I say when she picks up. "I have some bad news. Something came up, and I can't make dinner tonight."

"Oh, that's fine. Thanks for telling me."

"That's it? I thought you'd be pissed."

"You mean because you're calling at five o'clock to cancel?"

Ouch. "Yes. I'm sorry."

"Seriously, don't worry about it. We're still on for July?"

She has been planning to come to San José during the All-Star break. "Of course. I can't wait."

"Me, neither. Take care, John."

I barely have time to dwell on the chilliness of her sign-off—"Take care"?—before Tiff's driver pulls into the players' lot. Behind the wheel of a black Town Car sits a man about my age with curly ginger hair and a pale, freckled complexion. He looks like a grown-up Ron Weasley. The window inches down and he says, "Mr. Adcock? I'm Keith. Miss Tate says hello. Get in."

# 14

Twenty minutes later, Keith leaves me at the door of Denver International's general-aviation terminal, a place I know from dozens of team charter flights. In many ways, I prefer the commercial terminal to the GA, because there are better stores and real people. Private-jet patrons are either rich or robotic, and they want to pretend that they're alone, traveling in a hydraulic tube where the rest of the world does not exist. There are no distractions in the GA terminal, no TVs or communal waiting areas. On the commercial side, you have crying babies and other annoyances, but it's far more colorful and fun. On the GA side, a sports team is about the most colorful group you're going to see.

As promised, the terminal's receptionist escorts me to a plane parked about fifty yards from the building. At the base of the jet's stairs, we're met by a tight little blonde with enormous eyes. She has the powerful but girlish mien of an Olympic gymnast, with a well-muscled undercarriage packed into a pair of pin-striped slacks. Her chest is as flat as a boy's under a cream-colored cashmere sweater.

The blonde smiles warmly at the receptionist, as if to say, *I'll take it from here.*

"My name is Erica. I'll be caring for you and Miss Tate tonight." The way she says "you and Miss Tate" makes it sound like we're a couple. I wonder if this is part of the script. "Miss Tate is in her stateroom. Can I get you anything to drink while you wait?"

"Soda water with lime, if you have it."

At the top of the stairs, I duck to enter the plane. The main cabin is surprisingly generic. I would have expected Tiff to decorate, or at least add some mood lighting. The walls and carpet are a bland beige, and the seats are the same gray leather recliners you see in off-the-shelf corporate jets. Maybe she's worried about resale value.

Erica invites me to sit, and I flip through the magazines on the galley table: *Sports Illustrated, GQ, Black Tail,* and *Hustler.* Thoughtful selections. Tiff knows her clientele.

Erica delivers my soda in a chilled highball glass.

"Erica," I say. "That's a flower, isn't it?"

Call it a dirty trick, but I've made it a point to remember not only names but also their meanings. I know which are flowers, which are colors, which are saints, and so on. It's not all that complicated; I'm surprised more guys don't make the effort.

"That's right," Erica says. "Most people assume it's the female version of 'Eric,' but actually it's 'heather' in Latin."

"Heather in Latin. I like that."

She smiles. "It's my e-mail address."

"At Gmail?"

She shoots me a look that says she knows what I'm doing. "How about you? What does your name mean?"

"What, 'John'? Pretty sure it just means 'man.' Maybe 'ordinary man.'"

"I meant 'Adcock.'"

"Oh, that I'd have to show you. But not here."

She smiles and shakes her head. This Erica has the routine down pat. I change my mind about Tiff's decor: the furniture may be boring, but she did the important things right.

A door opens in the wood-paneled rear wall, and Tiff walks out. It appears that the rumor about her mutability is true—she looks completely different from when we met in the bullpen in San José. Today her hair is black, pulled tight, and mounted atop her head in a neat chignon. A red silk flower rests behind her right ear. Her skin is much paler than I remember, although the blood-red lipstick helps with that. Her black gypsy dress, which flows all the way to the floor, has ruffles at the shoulders and a scoop-neck décolletage. Her perfume smells vaguely of grapefruit.

"Thanks for coming," she says, taking a seat in the recliner opposite mine. She sits on the chair as though it were a pedestal, legs crossed and hands folded neatly over her knees. Her posture is erect; her eyes are bright and clear. I feel overmatched.

"No trouble at all," I say. "Nice plane."

"You have an update?"

So it's like that: Business first, party later? Maybe no party? I can't read her.

"Turns out Ruiz has a sister."

Tiff purses her glossy lips. "That may be. He said his whole family was being held hostage in Havana—"

"She's not in Cuba. She's here, in Denver."

"How do you know?"

"We met last night at a restaurant. She and Ruiz were there together. I went over to say hello, to introduce myself, but Ruiz wouldn't talk."

Tiff nods. "That makes sense. I told you, he's not allowed to speak with anyone outside the Rockies organization."

"Except you."

"Except me, correct."

"Well, his sister was happy to talk. Enriqueta is her name. She told me lots of things—for example, that she wasn't aware her family was being held at gunpoint. Also that, as far as she knows, Yonel has plenty of money."

"That's probably just her perspective. Cuba is a very poor country."

"Well, she's staying at the Ritz-Carlton."

"You followed her?"

"I did a thorough investigation."

Tiff smiles. "I see. Tell me what she looks like."

I give a basic physical description. When I get to the mismatched eyes, Tiff shifts in her chair.

"Is something wrong?" I ask.

"Yonel once told me about a woman with eyes like that. She's an associate of the Venezuelans. They call her La Loba."

The wolf. I think about those climactic minutes in the hotel room, staring into those crazy eyes. I remember also how interested she was in Tiff. "Do you know her?"

"Only by reputation. She's a contract killer."

"A hit woman?"

"Yes, but that doesn't make sense here. Why would she be out for dinner with Yonel if she were trying to kill him?"

"Maybe she wasn't trying to kill him," I say. "Maybe she's branching out. Maybe she's handling negotiations for the Venezuelans. Maybe she tags along to make sure he doesn't speak to anyone. Or maybe, I don't know . . . maybe they're involved?"

"I don't think so," Tiff says. "She might be appealing, but she's a professional killer. Who would agree to lock themselves in a room with her and turn out the lights? Yonel isn't stupid."

I feel my dick shrivel. "It's just a theory."

"Your theory is that La Loba is handling Yonel?"

"Could be. Something else happened today."

Tiff frowns. "You hit Yonel. I saw the clip on ESPN. What were you thinking? You could have hurt him."

"Not that. I got a call this afternoon, a disguised voice on a blocked number. Whoever it was knows I'm working the case. They said they have information I may find useful. I'm supposed to meet them tonight at eight."

"Where?"

"Some warehouse on West Forty-fourth Avenue."

"You need to be careful," Tiff says. "Do you have protection?"

I wonder how often she says that.

"What do you mean by protection?"

"You're in Colorado, Adcock. The crossing guards carry Bushmasters."

"I'm not going to carry a rifle."

"No, a pistol. Something quick and easy." She winks to make sure I'm on board. I say nothing, but she presses on anyway. "Go right now. Keith will take you."

"Now? It's already . . ." I look down at my watch. It's not even six o'clock. "Fine, call him."

Tiff taps a message on her phone. I realize she's right. I would feel more secure with a little something under my arm.

She crosses her legs and sits up straight. "She said she was his sister, huh? Well, I think it's fair to say they're not related."

"You never know," I say. "There's one in every family."

# 15

The shop is called National Standard Guns. It's open till midnight seven days a week. With its scuffed glass display cases and solicitous, slightly seedy clerks, it reminds me of the baseball-card shop where I used to spend my allowance in middle school. "Anything I can help you with?" says the clerk by the door. He's a dead ringer for Randy Johnson, nearly seven feet tall, with the same long nose and Yosemite Sam mustache. For a minute I believe he might be the Big Unit himself, before I remember reading somewhere that Johnson has taken up photography in his old age. Cameras, firearms—I was close.

"My friend here would like to purchase his first weapon," Keith says. I let the driver come inside with me, not only because I could use the advice (Keith claims to be a firearms expert) but because it felt mean to say no. He was so enthusiastic—like a toddler at a construction site. "I'm Keith, by the way." Keith and the Big Unit shake hands. The clerk's name turns out to be Keith as well. They have a chuckle about that, and then they get down to business. Within five minutes, we've established that I'm looking for a handgun, no modifications, and that I would prefer something new and reliable, given my lack of experience.

"You do know how to fire a weapon, correct?" Big Unit looks at me over the smoked lenses of his glasses.

"He does," answers Driver Keith.

"Yes, I do," I add, because I feel like I should answer for myself, and because it's true. Growing up, I would often visit family in Redlands, which back then was just orange groves and trailer trash. My cousins had a little firing range behind their house where my uncle would let us shoot his .22 target pistol, a shiny chrome number with a long barrel and elaborate scrolling on the stock. I always liked target practice. It was like pitching, without all the effort.

"Why don't you hold this and see how it feels?" The clerk hands me a squared-off pistol with a black matte finish. "That's your standard Glock nine."

"Standard is your specialty," I say.

Both Keiths look at me.

"It's the name of the store," I explain.

Humor, it turns out, is not appreciated at National Standard Guns. Smiles are okay, but only as reactions to the great and awesome power of the weapons for sale. I heft the Glock and stare down its barrel. ("Point it away from me, fella," Big Unit says. "Like this.") Then Keith the driver takes a turn. He grins as he holds the weapon at arm's length. The romance surrounding firearms in this town freaks me out. Deranged teenagers open fire in high schools and movie theaters here with such regularity that it's practically an annual season. It makes me wonder if Tiff's driver isn't a kind of civic booster sent to indoctrinate me.

"This is great," I say. "You sell bullets, too?"

"You don't want to see any others?" the driver says. "They've got three-fifty-sevens, revolvers, looks like a pretty good selection of convertible semiautos—"

"An excellent selection," Big Unit corrects.

"No, just this one, please." I pull out my wallet and draw out the first card I find. I expect the odyssey to end here. This is where Big Unit tells me that there's a waiting period, that I can buy the gun today but can't take it away till Monday, or next Saturday, or whatever it is. I should have asked about this up front, but I decided to play along, just in case. Maybe it's like getting carded, with some discretion left to the salesman.

Big Unit takes the credit card and asks to see my driver's license, which he hands to an associate. Then he tells me the price. It's much less than I was prepared to pay.

"That includes ammunition?"

"Two boxes are included, and you get a ten-percent discount if you buy more today."

"You should buy more," Keith suggests. "Ten percent is excellent."

The two Keiths seem to be working together. It reminds me of the time I went to India on an exhibition tour with my college team. The taxi drivers would agree to take you to the Taj Mahal, and then, on the way back to your hotel, they'd recommend stopping at the very finest rug shop in all of Agra, which I learned later meant that it gave taxi drivers the very finest kickbacks for delivering leads. Maybe Keith the driver gets a free box of ammo for every two I buy?

"One box is enough," I say. Again, I wait for Big Unit to shut me down. Instead, he nods and takes my card to the cash register, where he rings up the sale and rips off a neat little white receipt for me to sign. In the meantime, one of his associates has polished the gun, removed its tag, and wrapped it up in a neat quilted bag with a zipper. He hands me the gun, along with my ID.

"That's it?" I ask.

"You need something else? Targets, maybe?"

"I just thought, you know, that there was a waiting period?"

"Not in Colorado!" the driver says.

"No way," says Big Unit. "Not now and not ever. It's called the Second Amendment, and we take it real seriously here." The other clerks in the room, who have been listening the whole time, murmur their concurrence.

"There's no background check?"

"It's done," Big Unit says. "My colleague ran your license."

When we get back to the car, Keith asks if I'd like to sit up front.

"I'm okay in the back," I say. "But I would like to get some dinner. Do you know of anything around here?"

"You like meat? There's this all-you-can-eat Brazilian place around the corner. You know churrascarias? They carve it for you right at the table. Bloody as hell, just the way I like it."

# 16

I'm not sure what it says about American society, but I feel instantly safer once I have the pistol in my hands. I had planned to stuff it in the waistband of my pants, but when I explain this to Keith at dinner, he says I'm just asking to shoot my dick off. He gives me one of the extra shoulder holsters (there are multiple) in the trunk of his car. When he drops me off at a quarter to eight, I feel safer but more confused than I did when I left the ballpark. On the one hand, I'm better prepared. On the other, I feel like the city of Denver is trying to cajole me into killing someone.

The sun has gone down. The area is well lit from the street-lights. Keith leaves me a few blocks away so I can get my bearings before I show up for the meeting. He gives me his number and insists that I call when I'm done. I sense that he wants to stick around, that he's worried Tiff will give him hell if anything bad happens to me. I tell him to stay close. I won't be long.

Although there are no other pedestrians on Forty-fourth Avenue, the street is not deserted. Trucks rumble past at a regular clip, two or three a minute. The address in question no longer has any signs on its front door. The photo on the mapping app must have been old, or else the property recently changed hands. I recognize the loading dock, wide enough for two trailers. Next to that is a man-door with the address tacked up in crooked black numerals. The lone dusty window has its blinds drawn. With nine millimeters of confidence in my armpit, I walk up to the door and knock. There is no answer.

I check my phone and make sure that I have the right address. I do, but it's still early, ten till eight, so I go around back. The lighting is poor in the alley, and it takes me a minute to discern which door corresponds to my building. Turns out it doesn't matter, because all the doors are locked. I consider shooting off the knobs—that's something I can do now!—but it feels extreme. Maybe later, I tell myself, even though I know I didn't buy this gun to shoot doorknobs. Rifles may have other legitimate uses, but a handgun has only one: killing people.

I return to the front of the building and cross the street. In between two loading docks I find a dark niche, where I sit down and wait. Eight o'clock comes and goes. At eight-fifteen, there's still no activity in the warehouse. Then, finally, at eight-thirty, a black Suburban pulls up in front. A figure in loose black clothes and a black knit beanie jumps out of the passenger's door. Something about the way he walks feels familiar. He leaps up the steps to the front door, punches in a code, and steps inside. A light goes on behind the blinds.

Meanwhile, the driver throws the Suburban into reverse and backs up to one of the loading docks. When he's parked, the roll door comes up. The first guy is standing there, backlit by the empty warehouse. Rusted can lights dangle from the ceiling, illuminating a whole lot of nothing. The guy on the dock taps the roof of the Suburban. The driver gets out, and together they remove a long dark bag from the back of the truck. There's no mistaking that shape. The two men wrangle the body onto the dock with ease. They've obviously done this before.

They work quickly. In under a minute, they have hauled the

body inside and rolled the steel door down again. For a moment or two, I don't move from my hiding place. Now I know what's going on. The person who called me knew these guys would be coming here with a body around eight. He wanted me to see this. But why?

Then my phone buzzes.

*Don't go anywhere,* reads the new text. *Show's not done yet.*

I reach into my jacket and unsnap the strap on the holster. Five minutes elapse, then ten. I hear a strange noise coming from inside the warehouse, a high-pitched mechanical whistling. It starts, then stops, then starts again. The hoods appear to be occupied for the moment, so I decide to take my chances. I hurry across the street, duck behind the parked Suburban, then creep along the loading dock. I pause before the steps leading to the front door. I realize this is crazy: the thugs could open the door—either door—and find me here.

Then my phone buzzes again.

*Look in the window.*

The caller must be nearby. Or maybe he trained a camera on this spot? I tell myself it's a camera, because I really don't like the idea—the possibility—that he has a rifle scope trained on my back.

I leap up the steps and put my face to the window. There is a small gap between the blinds and the window frame. I can't see much, but I see enough: The driver is standing behind a piece of table-mounted power equipment. He's Latino, clean-shaven, with a scar on his upper lip from a crudely repaired cleft palate. The machine before him is a band saw with a stainless-steel table. It's a butcher's saw—I've seen them at Safeway. He pushes what looks like a rack of ribs through the saw, and the noise changes pitch, becoming higher as the blade cuts through bone. Blood pools on the steel table and drips onto the concrete floor. Near his feet stands a blue plastic kiddie pool filled with offal. I watch as he takes the resulting cuts—the chops?—and tosses them to the other guy, who is kneeling beside a long Coleman cooler.

Then I notice that the second guy isn't a guy at all. It's Enriqueta—or should I call her La Loba? Her hair is confined beneath the beanie, but the profile is definitely hers. She is intent on her work, trying to organize the chunks of meat so that they all fit into the cooler. She's so intent, in fact, that she isn't paying attention when her partner throws the last of the ribs, and it hits her in the face. She laughs, picks up the ribs, and chucks them back at the guy. He is not pleased and swears at her in Spanish.

Suddenly there's a loud bang. La Loba's posture stiffens. For a second I watch her, confused, and then my subconscious puts it all together. The noise was mine. It was my gun. I had been fondling it, stroking it absently in its holster. When I recognized La Loba, my hand must have twitched involuntarily and pulled the trigger.

I turn from the window and run. I tear down Forty-fourth, turn at the first corner, then run a few blocks and turn again. Eventually, the street dead-ends at a freeway embankment. I look around. I'm not being followed, for now.

There's a hole in the chain-link fence, and I squeeze through. Negotiating between crippled shopping carts and leaf bags full of stinking refuse, I find a place to crouch on the far side of a dusty azalea bush. I take out my phone and dial Keith. Headlights flash. I duck, burying the phone in my jacket. The car slows down but never stops. When it's gone I lift the phone to my ear.

"Keith—"

"Where are you, buddy?"

I locate a street sign and read out the block number.

"Hang tight," he says. "I'm five minutes away."

# 17

The best thing about day games is that you can have a whole day's worth of fun in the evening, then look down at your watch and see it's only 10:00 p.m. That's the situation I'm in when Keith drops me off in front of Connie's building. I called her from the car, but she didn't pick up, which means either she's angry at me or she's gone to bed. I'm exhausted and probably should go back to the team hotel to catch up on sleep—tomorrow is another day game—but it's Saturday night. I figure it's worth a shot.

I use the intercom to call up to Connie's apartment. She doesn't answer so I shoot her a text to say I'm here, that I'll be waiting in the bar downstairs if she's interested in making up. I decide to give her half an hour. I'll try the buzzer again before I leave.

The restaurant on the ground floor of her building has a retro speakeasy theme, with wood-paneled walls and cast-iron pipes hanging from the ceiling. The cocktails, which cost fifteen bucks and take fifteen minutes to make, have names like Sopwith Camel and Gin Van Landingham. At this hour, there's a kind of shift change going on among the clientele. A few tired-looking couples linger over espresso and cake crumbs, milking the babysitter for the last few precious moments. One by one their tables turn over to the party crowd, who are not necessarily younger than the date-night parents but certainly more energetic. That or they're well into the evening's first eight ball.

I take a seat at the bar, where most of the drinkers are sitting in silence, swiping at their cell phones. I think of the drunks in Joey's Big Sky, the bar where I met Mags. Hard to believe that was only a couple of days ago. This is a different crowd, to be sure, but maybe they're not as different as you'd think. I would expect this place to be filled with young people look-ing for love. These folks seem interested only in their phones. Izzy tells me that at her high school the most useful distinction is not between heterosexuals and homosexuals but between those who are sexual and those who are not. The abstainers call themselves "aces," short for "asexuals." "Ace is the new bi," Izzy informed me the other day on our call. The existence of these voluntarily castrated teenagers makes me sad. It reminds me of those punks who used to dye their hair gray, I guess as a fashion statement. I want to shake these kids and tell them there's plenty of time to be gray and abstinent. When you're young, dye your hair green and fuck your brains out—that's what being young is for.

Then I see someone I know at the end of the bar. It takes me a minute to place him, but only because he's out of con-text. It's Jock Marlborough, the Bay Dogs' radio play-by-play man. Jock is about a hundred pounds overweight, most of it bunched around the middle like a biscuit wrap. He's seated on the bar stool, his sagging flanks threatening to lap his ass; the only impediment is a blue-and-yellow Bay Dogs polo shirt. His wide, flat head is crowned by a tortured flaxen comb-over that must occupy most of his mornings. In an era where the shaved-head look has made balding nearly painless, I have never understood Marlborough's insistence on cultivating the style of a rabbi from 1979. Sure, he's old-fashioned—baseball announcers are all traditionalists at heart—but respecting tradition doesn't have to mean repeating mistakes. Tiff Tate, if she were here, would be moved to take his case pro bono.

I walk up and say hello.

"Adcock!" There's real surprise behind his narrow brown eyes. "You're the last person I expected to see here."

"Why's that, Jock?"

"No reason, just that the team hotel isn't nearby, and . . . well, I suppose you could say the same about me, couldn't you?"

His voice, I must say, is beautiful: every consonant in place, every vowel opened to its fullest potential. His dynamic range is extraordinary, moving from the dry business of earned-run averages and on-base percentages to the soaring height of his home-run call: "A high drive to deep right-center, Tucker goes back, to the track, to the waaall . . . *Auf-wieder-SEHEN!*" The last syllable cascades in pitch as the ball plunges into the crowd. This perfection is no accident. The home-run call is the trademark of a play-by-play man, and a memorable one takes years to develop. Marlborough likes to say he was born with the voice, but I tend to think that's impossible. None of us were born with our professional skills. I was blessed with a strong and resilient left arm, but everything I know about pitching I learned through hard work and repetition. I can imagine Jock Marlborough as a teenager locked in his bedroom with a Dictaphone, narrating the muted ballgame on the grainy TV, masturbating during the commercials, a bag of Cool Ranch Doritos between his knees, rewinding the tape to scrutinize his performance. Like most people who rise to the top of their professions, he focused on his one special talent to the exclusion of other kinds of development. Jock's voice is the finest of musical instruments, but it's like a Stradivarius in a pasteboard case. You'd think eventually he'd start to give a shit how he looks. At any rate, you can see why he never made the jump to TV.

I order a draft beer. Jock asks the bartender for another Canadian whiskey, neat.

"What brings you to this part of town?" I ask.

Jock rolls his eyes, and for the first time I notice he's trashed. "I'm on a date, if you can believe it. There's this app where you swipe women's faces and it matches you up. I was supposed to meet someone named Sharon here, but she never showed."

"I didn't know you were dating."

"New thing," he says. "Wife asked me to leave. Said she'd moved on, tired of being married to a ship captain. . . ." Even when he's drunk, Jock's pronunciation is crisp. The dropped subjects are the only tell. "No idea who he is. Guess I'll find out soon enough."

"Remind me—you have kids?"

"Two girls grown up and flown away. Always preferred their mother. No sympathy for old Dad, not that I deserved any. Missed their whole lives, practically. And for what, a golden mike and a pat on the ass? I'll be honest with you, Adcock, I'm not sure it's been worth the sacrifice."

The Hall of Fame inducts one or two announcers every year, and Jock's name is regularly mentioned as a candidate. He'll get the nod soon. The Hall of Fame. He's being too hard on himself.

"You've given them a good life. The girls went to college, right?"

"Stanford."

"Both of them?"

"Summa cum laude, ex officio, ad nauseam."

"Well, you had a big role in that, even if you weren't always there to see it happen."

It feels good to say these things, though I'm not sure who I'm reassuring, Jock or myself.

The bartender arrives with Jock's whiskey, and he clutches the tumbler in his stubby fingers. "Don't know about you, Adcock, but the death of our friend Magnusson has me twisted up inside. There but for the grace of God, et cetera." He raises his glass. "A toast to Erik Magnusson, premature explorer of the land we will one day call home, maybe sooner than we think."

We clink and drink. "How well did you know Magnusson?" I ask.

"We kept in touch," Jock says. "Decent guy. Uncommonly decent, if you know what I mean. Didn't deserve that business with his wife. She wanted everything. He never went into too much detail, but I know he was struggling financially. I offered to loan him some cash."

"Did he accept?"

"He said he'd think about it." Jock pauses. "But then this happened."

We observe another moment of silence, and then Jock grunts. "Why does anyone get married? We all know how it turns out. Hey!"—he says brightly, as if realizing only now who he's been talking to—"You have experience with this!"

For a moment I think he means divorce. But he's talking about my side work, the matrimonial investigations I'm known for. "I know a little."

"Going on thirty years I've been doing this job, and suddenly, now, my wife is sick of it? I have no proof that she's fooling around, but, you know, if it walks like a duck and talks like a duck . . . I think that's Shakespeare, by the way."

"Is it?"

"You can help me."

"Jock, I'm sorry, but my plate is full right now."

"Any chance of persuading you to work overtime?" Jock's eyes are bloodshot, his old-man brow knotted together like a golden retriever's. I see a man chewed up by this game, a man who accomplished exactly what he set out to do, only to discover that it wasn't worth the price he paid. I don't have the time or the mental space to take on another case, but how can I turn him down?

"I'll need your home address," I say, "and whatever you can tell me about your wife—any hobbies, clubs, professional organizations."

"Professional organizations?"

"When a wife takes a man on the side, it's almost always somebody she knows in another context. Women don't generally sleep with strangers."

"Is that supposed to make me feel better?"

"It's not supposed to make you feel anything, it's just the truth."

"Beauty is truth," he says, "truth beauty."

"That's Keats."

"Adcock!"

"I'm dating a librarian. I'm surrounded by books."

"Lucky you. My wife is a real estate agent. I'm surrounded by assholes!"

# 18

When I finally get back to the team hotel, it's one-thirty in the morning. Jock felt it was only right to give Sharon till closing, so I left him at the bar. It's been an evening of disappointments. Connie never answered her door. The only trigger getting pulled tonight belongs to my new Glock, and that was an accident. Luckily, the fallout from my error is minimal: a dime-sized hole through the back panel of my jacket and a powder burn on the lining. As Plaxico Burress will tell you, carrying a piece is no easy feat, especially if you want to look cool. All night I've been worried that it would go off again, so I've tried to keep my right elbow six inches off my hip. I must have looked like a gimp on the barstool.

I open the door to my room, and cold air pours into the hall. I turn on the light and try to remember the location of the thermostat. I turned it up last night, but the maid must have reset it to the industry-standard "meat locker" setting. As I'm looking for the controller, my phone rings. I'm hoping it's Connie, but it turns out to be my daughter. I try not to sound disappointed.

"Izzy." I look at the clock. "Why aren't you in bed?"

"Dad, jeez, I stay up much later than this."

"It's twelve-thirty your time."

"Yeah, so? It's Saturday night."

"Does your mother know you're on the phone?"

Ginny, my ex, finally allowed me to buy Isabel a cell phone when she finished ninth grade. I had been lobbying to get her a phone for years, mainly so that Izzy and I could communicate without having to go through her mother. But now that she's got the thing, I wonder if Ginny was right to resist. I can't remember what time my parents turned off the phone at night, but I'm pretty sure it was before twelve-thirty.

"I'm not allowed to call my friends after eight-thirty, but Mom says I can call you anytime."

"Does she know you're on the phone right now?"

"She's asleep." She pauses. "Do you want me to hang up?"

"You don't have to hang up, but you need to respect your mother's rules. As long as you're living in her house, you need to be respectful."

Izzy breezes past this advice. "You're at Connie's, right?" She and Connie hit it off last winter, when Izzy visited Colorado during Christmas vacation. We took her to Vail. Izzy knows how to ski, but the highlight of her trip was conspiring with Connie, inventing nicknames for their favorite ski instructors, getting spa treatments, and sitting in the sauna together. I felt left out most of the time, but it was good to see Izzy so happy.

"Actually, tonight I'm at the hotel by myself."

"Poor Daddy . . ." This is a new stance she's been testing out lately, treating her father like a pet—I'm sure it's just another way she's stretching those adolescent muscles, a necessary step in her psychological development, but I don't like it. I get patronized enough by her mother. I don't need it from her protégée.

"So what's on your mind, or are you just calling to say hello?"

"I'm wondering if you're going to make it to my dance performance. It's on August—"

"I know when it is." My voice is louder and more defensive than I intended. "It's on my calendar, and I'm going to be sending you happy thoughts. But the team is in Cincinnati that weekend. I told you this months ago."

"You said you'd try to make it."

"I didn't say that."

"You did, I remember!"

This is another new habit: asking for favors she knows I can't grant. This one hurts even more than the patronizing. There isn't much I can't give my daughter, but during the season, my time is not my own. My schedule is determined a year in advance and set in stone. Worse than stone: it's printed on tickets. Izzy knows the deal. I've been playing professional baseball her whole life. Except on very rare occasions, her father has never been able to attend midsummer dance recitals, or midsummer anything. I understand it must be hard for her. All of her friends' fathers, even the corporate lawyers and Hollywood power brokers, have some wiggle room in their schedules, whereas I have none. Which sucks, and I feel guilty as hell about it, but it does no good to beg.

"I would never have said that, Isabel."

"But, Daddy, I thought that maybe this one time . . ." She stops with a grunt.

I met my ex-wife in the jock dorm at Cal State Fullerton. I suppose it's a kind of poetic justice that the only child of two Division I athletes would eschew team sports for a sequined leotard. But I know that grunt. That grunt makes me smile. Underneath that leotard is a beast with my DNA.

"It doesn't have to be like this," she insists. "Mom says you can retire anytime you like."

"I don't know what your mother means by that, but I certainly don't need her permission to retire. The fact is that I play baseball because I want to, and because a major-league team wants me to play for them. I know my job puts you in a difficult situation. I feel horrible that I can't be at your recital.

But you have to understand that we have it good, better than ninety-nine-point-nine percent of the world. My job may be frustrating to you, but think of everything it provides. Your school, for instance—someone has to pay for that."

"I know, Daddy," she says, suddenly contrite.

"The good news is that when I do retire I'll be around more than you can imagine. Probably more than you want." I feel bad for breaking her down. She's still so fragile.

"But when? Mom says you've saved enough money already."

"Enough for what?"

"Enough to retire."

"Suppose I did. How would you feel about having an unemployed dad?"

"I'd be fine with it. Kelsey's dad got laid off two years ago, and he's still unemployed. He had to sell his car, but it's fine. He picks her up from school sometimes."

"On foot?"

"Yeah. They stop at Jamba Juice on the way home."

I wish it were that simple. Maybe it is for Kelsey's dad. Maybe he's fine picking his way through the housewives in the after-school throng. I wish that could be me, but I need more. I don't feel good if I'm not working, and even baseball isn't enough sometimes.

"Sorry, Iz. I'll be there for your Christmas show."

"The Christmas show is for babies. It's the same routines every year. Summer is when we perform new material. It's when we grow as dancers!"

When they grow as dancers? Did she really just say that? It sounds like cult dogma. Parents complain about the scourge of kids' travel baseball teams—the early-morning drives, the never-ending practices—but what about dance teams? They go year-round, too, and they colonize your daughter's brain.

"You'll just have to grow without me, as you have every summer since you were born. They're filming the show, right? Order a DVD, and we'll watch it together." I pause. "As for retirement, all I can promise is that you'll be the first to know."

"Should I just quit? Kelsey quit dance last year, and she says it was the best decision she ever made. Now she has time to relax."

"Izzy, being young isn't about relaxing. Right now you're healthy and you enjoy dancing, so you should do it as long as they'll let you. Or as long as your body holds up."

"Um, okay . . ."

"Look, I know how you feel. There are a million reasons to quit sports, and people love to recite them, especially as you get older, but this is your decision, understand?"

"I just wanted to see what you thought."

"I think you should keep dancing. That's my expert opinion."

"Really?"

"Really. Now get to bed."

"Okay."

"Talk to you tomorrow. I love you."

I turn off the lights and TV. Then I'm on my back for what seems like hours, wondering if I'm doing right by Isabel. Maybe I should retire. In three years she'll be out of the house, off to college and an independent life. What I really want is some balance, maybe a month off every summer. I'd take a pay cut, or work in February instead, but unfortunately that's not possible if I want to keep this job. Life is full of irreversible choices. Popular wisdom holds that it's never too late to change careers, to right your wrongs, to stop drinking or smoking or whatever, but in my opinion that's bullshit. Some decisions set your course forever. When Izzy was born, I was playing in the minor leagues, struggling with my command, and trying to develop that third pitch everybody said I needed. I made a choice to shut my family out and concentrate on my game, and it worked: I made it to the majors within a year. But I lost my marriage, and I set a course that would cause me to miss my daughter's childhood. I will never get that back, no matter what steps I take right now. I could retire tomorrow, but it wouldn't restore what I've lost.

I feel bad about Izzy. And Connie. I even feel bad about Tiff Tate. Is there anyone else whose life I can ruin today? Anything else I can screw up? I survey the hotel room. I could throw the TV out the window. I could stuff a towel into the bathtub drain and start a flood. I'm only half kidding.

There's only one thing to do, and that's sleep. I brush my teeth halfheartedly, strip, and dig a tunnel into the drum-tight bedclothes. The room is still freezing, but I can live with it. I lie there for a while, tired as hell but restless. No sooner do I finally drift off than I am jolted awake by a knock at the door. I stagger out of bed and look through the peephole. It's a young African American in a business suit with a name tag bearing the hotel's logo.

I wrap a towel around my waist and open the door a crack, leaving the security latch fastened. "What do you want?" I croak.

"Mr. Adcock, right? Sorry to bother you, sir, but I have a letter. It was delivered by private courier yesterday with instructions to put it in your hand as soon as possible, but you never came in last night, so . . ."

"Give it to me."

As soon as the envelope passes through the crack, I slam the door shut—a dick move, maybe, but it's two o'clock in the morning.

I turn on the light. The envelope is standard size, plain white, bearing the words *Johnny Adcock—URGENT* in black Sharpie. I hold it up to the light. What am I checking for, exactly? It looks like a piece of paper. A letter. I tear it open and read:

*Dear Johnny,*

*I lied. I never got that anonymous call during spring training. I made that up, sorry. I wanted to warn you off, because nobody has time to get involved with some Caribbean asshole trying to beat the system. Am I right? It was a stupid idea. I'm not much older than you, but I guess I was trying to play daddy. Obviously you can handle your own business, and if you want to get involved with Ruiz, that's your prerogative.*

The letter is signed *Warm personal regards, Erik Magnusson,* which, given the context, feels both impersonal and strangely intimate. Mags is—was—weird like that. His mother raised him right, you might say.

I slip the letter back into the envelope. I have never received a letter from beyond the grave before. It's more frustrating than eerie. I can't help thinking that Magnusson might still be alive if he'd come clean with me the other night. Then again, maybe I'm being arrogant. What could I have done? Now that I know Magnusson was lying about the call, the case makes even less sense than it did before. The line about the *Caribbean asshole trying to beat the system* could refer to a Fausto Carmona–style name change, but how much credence should I give to a name scrawled idly on a whiteboard? I haven't heard back from Don Anibal in Cuba. Pascual Alcalá could be anyone.

My worry is that this letter still isn't the whole story. Maybe another letter will show up tomorrow, in which Mags tells me he lied about something else. Then what will I have?

This job would be so much easier if everyone told the truth. Then again, if everyone told the truth, I wouldn't have this job.

# 19

Today is the last of the three-game stand with the Rockies. Getaway day, we call it. First pitch today is at 1:00 p.m., and we'll be on the plane back to San José by six. The guys with families might even see their kids before they go to bed. On getaway day, you pack your bags before you leave for the park and drop them off in the lobby. I have a lot to do this morning, so I leave my bags with a yawning assistant a few minutes after eight. I walk out to the curb to meet Keith. I've decided that Uber is great, but nothing beats a full-time driver—especially when someone else is picking up the tab.

I jump into Keith's Town Car and give him Connie's address just as my phone rings. Someone else is up early. This one is a surprise. "Todd?"

My agent, Todd Ratkiss, is a decent guy as agents go—a sweaty, freckled version of Jerry Maguire. He's in his early fifties and already on his third family. I don't understand why he doesn't just get fixed. I get his desire to have a new woman every once in a while, but the guy has had toddlers in his house for twenty years.

In the background, I hear the chatter of cable news and the churning of a treadmill.

"Where the hell are you, Adcock? I've been calling all night!"

This is one of Todd's favorite expressions. It doesn't actually mean he's been up all night. He certainly hasn't been calling me. "We got a love note from the commissioner's office. You've been suspended."

"For Yonel Ruiz?"

"What happened out there? I saw the video, and I can't figure it out. Was it payback for something I don't know about?"

"Ball slipped," I say.

"That's how it's going to be, huh?"

"That's how it's going to be."

"Well, you have twenty-four hours to appeal, if that's what you want to do. My advice is to take the suspension today. With the scheduled off-day on Monday, you'll have a nice little vacation. Unpaid, of course."

Ratkiss works on commission, taking 4 percent of everything I earn. At $9,300 per game ($1.5 million over a 162-game season), Ratkiss stands to lose about $370 if I take the suspension. That's not much for a man who lives in a house with seven bathrooms, but it's something. A whole week of dog grooming, even.

"Fine," I say, "but I'm not happy about it."

Ratkiss laughs. "I don't know why you would be!"

"You were trying to make it sound like fun."

"You know what you need, Johnny? You need to blow off some steam. You're running too hot. I see it in your body language on the mound. How about this? The Bay Dogs are in L.A. at the end of the month—how about I take you out? We'll get some drinks, maybe some maguro. You know what that is, right? The word literally means 'tuna,' but in Japan it's also slang for a woman's—"

"I know what it means."

"It'll be fun." Ratkiss lives in Newport Beach, but he keeps a condo for entertainment in one of the new high-rises downtown. I've only heard about it, never been invited. I take a moment to imagine a pied-à-terre decorated for Todd: the walls are covered in mirrors, every piece of furniture is a waterbed. Shakers of salt, pepper, and cocaine on the kitchen table. It sounds exhausting.

"Maybe, Todd. We'll see."

"Let me know. Call Debbi, she'll set everything up."

Debbi is Todd's assistant. She's been with him longer than his last two wives. Nobody knows the trouble she's seen. I hope he pays her well.

"I'll notify the club and the commissioner's office," he says. "Remember that while you're on suspension you're not allowed to be in the dugout or press box during the game. Also, I'd advise you not to speak with the media."

"Got it. Any other advice?"

He exhales heavily. "Honestly? I just wish you'd keep yourself out of trouble. Is that too much to ask?"

"Probably, but don't let that stop you from trying."

# 20

"Another booty call, huh?" Keith winks in the rearview mirror. I forgot that he dropped me at Connie's last night.

"Not exactly. Mending fences."

"Oh." Keith nods and doesn't pursue this line of questioning any further. A good driver knows when to shut up. Wing nut or not, Keith is a good one. I plan to commend him to Tiff.

He leaves me at the curb, and I dial Connie on the intercom. The phone rings a full minute before I hang up. I realize it was shitty to cancel on her, but do I really deserve the silent treatment? I wasn't with another woman last night—and, besides, Connie knows I see other women. Maybe she's not completely aware of how many women, or which women, or how soon after sleeping with her I might have bagged a certain wolf-eyed Latin hit woman, but my point stands: I'm no angel. I thought she understood.

The sidewalk tables in front of the bar have been pushed together and secured like a chain gang. I pace the deserted sidewalk, kicking chunks of pine mulch back into the planters around the aspens. Maybe Connie isn't angry at all. Maybe I'm overreacting. Maybe she's just out jogging or doing some early-morning shopping. That doesn't explain why she won't answer the phone.

Ever since I got that anonymous call yesterday, a pebble of fear has been rattling around in my stomach, nagging me to pay attention. Both Ruiz and La Loba saw me with Connie the other night. It wouldn't have taken too much work on their part to figure out who she was and how to get to her. It's a possibility, that's all, but at this point I wouldn't put it past either of them.

Another thing: Tiff hired me to protect Ruiz, but I feel like things have gotten switched up. Am I protecting Ruiz, or is he the danger? I'll say this: he keeps strange company for an innocent man.

I text Keith and ask him to come back. He can't have gone too far in ten minutes. Then I lean against the glass door of the bar and slide down until my ass hits the pavement. Secretly, I hope that, in the time it takes Keith to get here, Connie will walk out of her apartment building and we can put this incident behind us. Honestly, I'm not looking for makeup sex: at this point I'd be happy just to know she's alive.

A minute later, someone does walk out of the building, but it's not Connie—it's a neighbor I recognize from last winter, Barry or Barney or something, a divorced mining engineer in his fifties. He travels a lot for work, but when he's in town, he's always hanging around the building. He and Connie have keys to each other's apartments so they can water plants, feed cats, that sort of thing. He has an obvious crush on her. She finds him sweet and harmless, but I've always thought he could be a serial killer, with his shiny thinning hair and glasses with photochromic lenses. Today he's wearing a sky-blue polo tucked into khaki shorts and a pair of boat shoes so squeaky clean this might be their maiden voyage.

I spring to my feet and catch the door before it closes. "Hey there!" I greet Barry/Barney.

"Is that John?" The neighbor squints. "Welcome back, friend! How have you been?"

"Busy. It's the middle of the season. I'm in town for a weekend series."

"Of course you are!"

"I'm so glad I caught you. I was wondering if you could help me surprise Connie."

"She's not home?"

"She went to the gym. We were supposed to meet for breakfast, but I had this team meeting that went long. . . ." My story is far from airtight; I'm hoping the neighbor's sense of romance will inspire him to go with the flow.

"Let me guess," he says with a conspiratorial smirk, "you want me to let you into the apartment so you can make coffee and scramble some eggs, and then, when she arrives from the gym all sweaty and flushed, you will wrap her up in your arms and lift her off to paradise?"

"Something like that, yeah."

"Fantastic!" He pauses. "However, there is one problem."

"What's that?"

"Well, there's the matter of yesterday's misbehavior."

How does this guy know I stood her up? I guess they're closer than I realized. "I tried to call," I say, "but the game went long, and we're not allowed to use our phones—"

"I'm referring to your behavior on the mound. You hit our young Cuban star with an unprovoked beanball."

"Do you follow baseball?"

"Are you surprised?"

"No, I just . . . Connie never mentioned it."

"It's a private passion. I have followed the Rockies religiously since their inception. And I have to say, this Cuban man is the most promising development since Tulowitzki."

"He's a beast, for sure."

"I understand you may not like him, but surely you recognize that he deserves the chance to compete without the threat of decapitation?"

"Of course I do." I try to fill my voice with contrition, bowing my head before continuing. "Can I confess something?"

The neighbor's eyes shine. "Absolutely."

"You probably know it's against the rules to throw at a batter. Pitchers never admit they hit a guy on purpose, but most of the time it's not an accident. Usually, it's payback for something the other team did."

"I've read about this. Baseball's unwritten code of conduct."

"That's it. I'm going to tell you something, but I need to be absolutely sure you can keep it secret. You can't tell anyone. Not even Connie."

"John, most of the people in my life have no idea I follow baseball. You can trust me."

I lower my voice. "Remember Ruiz's home run on Friday?"

"Second inning, one-two pitch from Wheeler, I believe it was a slider?"

He pays attention—perfect. "So you remember how he flipped his bat?"

"What showmanship!" The neighbor grins.

"Well, we don't like that sort of thing. Pitchers especially. You don't see us throwing our gloves when we strike someone out. The code says you don't celebrate a home run, you just run the bases and take a seat on the bench. So, when a guy like Ruiz does that to my buddy . . ."

"Then you hit him."

"Ruiz knows the deal. He's making a choice when he flips his bat. Getting popped in the back is a price he's willing to pay."

"I see."

"And, for the record, if I'd wanted to hit him in the head, I would have. I was aiming for his back."

The neighbor nods nervously. "Yes, you must have been."

"So does that help? Do you understand the situation a little better now?"

We take the elevator up to Connie's floor, and I wait as the neighbor fetches her key from his apartment. After he unlocks the door, he holds it for a moment before letting me in. "Let me ask you something, Johnny. Once you hit Ruiz for his indiscretion with the bat, is the score settled? How do you know that one of our pitchers won't hit you in retaliation?"

"That's up to Ruiz. Watch his next home run. See if he flips the bat."

"I had no idea the code was real," the neighbor says meekly.

I slip into the apartment and shut the door. Through the peephole, I watch him retreat into his apartment. I hope I didn't rock his world too badly, especially because it was a lie: the code is real, but Ruiz wasn't due to get popped. Bat flips aren't as controversial as they once were. Yesterday's "misbehavior" was all mine. I hit Ruiz by my own free will.

The air in Connie's apartment is still and warm. Cozy, as usual. But when I turn around and face the living room, it's like my worst nightmare has come true. Blood has been sprayed over the sofa and smeared against the walls. More blood has pooled under the coffee table. Directly above me, a woman in a familiar knee-length asymmetrical dress hangs by her neck from a rope.

I open my mouth to scream.

Then I look closely. It's not a body but a vinyl blow-up doll, a sex toy. It's hanging low and heavy on the noose, more like a sandbag or an Italian cheese than a balloon. I realize that the doll is filled with liquid. Blood, or something standing in for blood, is leaking from a tiny hole in the doll's left foot.

The details are eerily accurate: The dark wig has the same cut and styling Connie wore the night before last. The eyeglasses are a close match, and there's a library book taped under one arm. It's an odd effect; I can't decide if it's meant to be horrifying or *Rocky Horror*. Despite the costume, the doll cannot overcome that fuck-me face, the eternally puckered mouth, the innocent anime eyes. It's like Betty Boop dressed as a librarian for Halloween. But when you consider how this must have looked to Connie, any irony drops away. A line of blood runs from the doll's mouth over her chin and down her neck. Effigy—that's what this is called. Connie has been murdered in effigy.

I bend down and touch the "blood" on the sofa. It's dry. The puddle under the coffee table is still sticky in the middle, where the drip hits, but the rest is congealed. It feels like latex paint.

I spin around and reach for the door, but my hip knocks the edge of the unsteady little table where Connie drops her keys and purse. The table falls over, and the surprise—I'm jacked on adrenaline—knocks me backward against the hat rack on the opposite side of the doorway. The hat rack topples over, and now I'm on my ass in a sea of coats and farmers'-market tote bags, hoping the neighbor is back in his apartment out of earshot.

Then, on the floor, I see something, a single sheet of paper that must have fallen off the table. It's an itinerary from an airline website. The flight departed yesterday, at 3:05 p.m. The destination was San Francisco, and the passenger, printed plainly in black ink, was OCONNELL, CONSTANCE/MS.

# 21

"Airport, huh?" Keith twists around in the driver's seat. His orange hair is lit up like a halo by the mile-high sun. "Don't you have a game?"

"My arm hurts, so they're sending me ahead."

Since Keith raises no objection to this logic, I proceed with my plan. "I have a present for you." I reach up and hand him back his holster—and, inside it, the Glock.

"Mr. Adcock, I can't take this."

"Sure you can. You don't have to tell Tiff."

"No, I mean, I really can't. We'd have to file paperwork to get the ownership transferred. It's a huge pain in the ass."

"You can accept it as a gift, or you can watch me throw it in the river. Those are the options. I have no luggage to check, and I can't take it on the plane with me."

"The river? Christ, no . . ."

"Your choice."

After a long pause, he says, "How about this? I'll hold this weapon for you, and next time you're in Denver, I can give it back."

"Like a gun share? I like it. It's Zipcar for firearms."

"If that's how you want to think of it, sure. But, technically, it's still your gun."

"Technically, yes."

"And legally?"

"Legally, it's also still mine."

He smiles. "You're a good guy, Adcock. Good things are coming to you, mark my words."

"I hope you're right."

He taps the holster on the passenger's seat. "Hope's got nothing to do with it."


The next flight to the Bay Area (San José, as it turns out) doesn't leave for two hours, so I take a seat near an unused gate and make some phone calls. First, of course, I try Connie. Still no answer. I don't know what to make of the fact that she left town without telling me. So much for the theory that she was angry because I stood her up: she herself was a thousand miles from Denver when we were supposed to meet for dinner. Her father lives in a small town north of San Francisco. I suspect that's where she went, but it still doesn't explain why she isn't answering my calls. Life in Healdsburg is slow, but they do have cell service.

With some time to kill, I decide to do some digging on Kitty Marlborough, Jock's allegedly unfaithful wife, following the leads he gave me last night. A Google search leads me to the website of the San Mateo County Association of Realtors. Apparently, Kitty Marlborough gave a presentation last night at a Marriott in Daly City, as part of a daylong training on changes to the county's zoning ordinances. Jock is lucky the meeting was held at a Marriott. Five minutes later, I have Ken Briggman on the phone—Ken is head of security for Marriott's Western region. We met several years ago, during a bomb scare at the team hotel in Seattle. Since then, I've cultivated him with tickets and club passes. Now it's time to pay the scalper.

"Is this Ken? Johnny Adcock here."

"Adcock! Long time, *hombre. Qué pasa?*"

Before I go any further, I have to explain that Ken Briggman is the whitest man I've ever met. His hair is the color of rice noodles, and his eyebrows are translucent. He's Mormon and lives in Salt Lake with his wife and six kids. I'm on his Christmas-card list. The glare from the eight blond heads is blinding.

"Got a favor to ask, Ken. A friend of mine has a problem with his mother. He thinks she's fooling around behind his dad's back."

"This another player?"

"A future Hall of Famer, as a matter of fact."

"No kidding. Is it Modigliani?"

"I can't give you the name, but I sure would appreciate your help."

Briggman turns serious. "Absolutely. What do you need?"

"There was an event last night at the Junípero Serra Marriott. . . ."

"Property 00564. Daly City, California. A hundred guest rooms plus a conference facility including an extensible ballroom and half a dozen breakout chambers."

"That's the place. If I send you a photo of someone, would you be able to find her on your security tapes?"

Briggman chuckles. "Officially, no, but—confidentially?— 00564 is one of three facilities in the region where we're piloting OmniSentry."

"OmniSentry?"

"It's a military-grade surveillance-and-analysis package. Multi-angle video, infrared filters, facial recognition. It's the same system they use at the Pentagon. The corporate guys in Maryland are considering it for deployment across all our conference facilities next fiscal year, but they wanted some site testing first. The vendor agreed to let us do it, but only under the condition that we do it silently. I guess they don't want it known that we've installed the system without federal clearance. See, because this was originally DOD technology, there are all kinds of clearances. . . ."

"I understand completely." (Not at all, but I don't have time for details.) "Can you find her if I tell you when and where she did a presentation? I'm interested to know where she went afterward, and with whom."

"You know," Briggman says, "this could actually be super-useful to us. I mean, the whole rationale behind the system deployment is to give us the capability to track persons of interest—as in suspicious characters, but also high-value targets like presidents and foreign heads of state, that kind of thing."

So Kitty Marlborough will get the head-of-state treatment. Not bad for a philandering realtor.

"You'll do it, then?"

"Like I said, officially, no. But send me the photo, and we'll see what falls onto my screen."

# 22

By late afternoon, I'm in downtown San José. My apartment is on the twenty-first floor of a new building a few blocks from the ballpark. For me, the five-minute commute makes this place a no-brainer, but most of my teammates prefer to rent homes in the hills, where the neighborhoods are full of culs-de-sac and pregnant wives in workout clothes. That I own my condo is even stranger; these days, ballplayers change teams so often that they rarely own real estate, except back where they grew up or in Florida or Arizona, one of the spring-training locations. I know guys whose "homes" are storage lockers in Tempe. Another guy belongs to a country club in Scottsdale but doesn't have a permanent address. "You can always find a hotel room," he says, "but not a tee time."

The apartment smells like cleaning solution. The housekeepers come once a week, whether or not I'm in town. Aside from a few personal artifacts (mostly in Izzy's room) and the fact that I own it, this place might as well be a hotel. But the sterility doesn't bother me. If you live on the road long enough, you learn to give up sentimental attachments to place.

I turn on the TV and watch my team getting thrashed in Denver. Baseball looks so neat and tidy on television, with the two dozen camera angles and all the relevant counts and scoring encapsulated in that corner display. Out on the field, you keep track of the count, the outs, and the runners on base, and that's it. At home you've got the players' statistics and history, the weight of all those numbers on the screen, plus whatever the announcers are saying. On the field it's almost silent between pitches, even on the mound. When you're pitching well, it feels like jogging, just you and your body, moving as you have trained it to move. This is what pitchers mean when they talk about finding their rhythm. It's about finding a way to be alone with yourself with forty thousand people looking on.

The Rockies triumph, 11–4, and the Adcockless Bay Dogs fall three games behind the Dodgers in the National League West. Skipper is not going to be happy. Nobody's going to be happy. I'm angry with myself, even if the loss is not my fault, because my anger isn't just about the loss. Ordinarily, I don't feel too bad when investigations turn sour—when the trail goes cold and I have to report failure to my client. Normally, I can just say: Well, what did you expect? I'm not a detective, I'm a relief pitcher! But today I'm not even a pitcher. I'm just a guy on his couch, watching baseball on TV. And this time the case touches me personally. I should be out searching for my girlfriend. I had every intention of getting on my bike and driving up to Sonoma to look for Connie, but I'm drained. The last twenty-four hours have been exhausting.

And then the impossible occurs.

The intercom buzzes. I mute the TV and go to the door. Through the fish-eye lens of the security camera, I see a woman with chin-length dark hair and fair skin. She's wearing glasses, a short skirt, and a tight-fitting sweater set from Benetton or H&M. The back of my neck tingles. The resolution on the tiny screen isn't very good, but when she looks up at the camera, the eyes are unmistakable. It's Connie.

I tap the button. The elevators in my building are fast, and she shouldn't have to wait long at this hour. What time is it, anyway? Five-thirty? It's unlike Connie to make a surprise visit. Then again, I believed it was unlike her to disappear without telling me.

The doorbell rings as I'm fiddling with the stereo, looking for something with female vocals, something emotional. Izzy sent me an album by a woman called St. Vincent, who has the face of Peter Pan and the hair of Albert Einstein. The music is interesting, lots of syncopated drums and processed guitar sounds. Not exactly soothing, but it will have to do for now.

I check my hair, my teeth, my fly. I open the door.

Standing in the hall, backlit by the lights from the elevator lobby, is not Constance O'Connell but Tiff Tate. The resemblance is uncanny: her cheeks have the same freckles, her hair the same color and texture. The makeup is Connie's, as is the reticent smile. The eyes must be contacts, but the color match is perfect. Still, there's no question it's Tiff. Her shoulders are wider than Connie's. She's fuller in the breasts and hips. The disguise isn't meant to be foolproof. It was meant to fool a security camera, and it passed that test handsomely. Tiff steps past me into my apartment. She takes it in with a sweeping glance.

"Nice place," she says. "Do you have any idea what this would cost in New York?"

"What are you doing here?"

She whirls around and gathers the front of my shirt in her fist. "I did a bad thing, Johnny." Her voice is full of sex, but her eyes are wet, like she's going to cry. "I was mean and inconsiderate, and it's eating me up inside."

"What are you talking about?"

Lifting my shirt with one hand, she slides the other down the front of my jeans. My body reacts as conditioned. (As I said, she looks a lot like Connie.)

"I screwed up," she says.

"What did you do?"

"Let me relax first," she says. "Bedroom's which way?"

She follows me into the master suite, where she pushes me onto the bed. We begin kissing, first softly, then with increasing force, until she is pulling my tongue deep into her mouth. I relieve her of the sweater and skirt. She's not wearing any underwear. I see that she is in shape, not ripped but attractive. Her breasts are larger than I expected and almost certainly natural, with wide, dark nipples that suggest—if I'm reading them correctly—that she may be dark-complexioned in her default configuration. She has no tan lines anywhere. I tug off my jeans, grab a rubber from the nightstand, and slide inside her. She moans hoarsely—I guess the Connie impersonation is over—and asks me to bite her nipples. It's like a magic trick: she comes right away. She allows me to finish, and I roll off.

"Feel better?" I ask when I've regained my breath.

"Yes, thank you."

"What's so horrible that you had to be hammered flat before you could tell me about it?"

Tiff sits up. There are bite marks on her areolae and her makeup is ruined, but she looks me straight in the eye, boring into me with tremendous concentration. She's either totally insane or the least self-conscious person on earth. "I'm in trouble," she says.

"With Ruiz?"

"With La Loba. I wasn't entirely honest about her. La Loba is not a contract killer. She's a smuggler."

"Like a human trafficker?" What if La Loba were the one turning the screws on Ruiz? What if she smuggled him off the island? That would explain their meeting in the restaurant in Denver.

"Well, her business is Cuban athletes. She has cornered the market."

"And?"

"And it's lucrative." Tiff goes quiet. Almost reverent. "Very lucrative."

I think private jet. I think disguises. Something clicks.

"Tiff."

Silence.

"You smuggled Ruiz out of Cuba."

Tiff smiles.

"And now La Loba wants to kill you to make a statement."

Her smile fades away, and I know I'm right.

As she puts on her clothes, Tiff tells me the story.

"Over the last couple of years, these Cubans and their handlers were coming to see me, and everything seemed fine and good until I got the players alone and they told me how much money they had to pay to get out—fifty to seventy-five percent of their salaries, after risking their lives. I realized I could do the same thing for a fraction of the price, and I could do it without any risk. Appearance is fluid and controllable, Johnny. I can manipulate it well. Call it a bit of personal and professional vindication. So I went to Cuba and found Yonel tearing up the league. Fifteen percent was all I'd take. Fifteen percent of his first contract, and no shark-infested seas, no Santería priests, no blackmail. Just a falsified passport, a plane ticket to Mexico, and a fashion-forward beard."

"And that's how it happened?"

"Pretty much. But I was naïve. Turns out La Loba's people have smuggled out every Cuban ballplayer who has escaped the island in the last ten years. When she found out I'd taken Yonel, she was furious. I got a call saying there was a bomb in my house in Boston. Then Yonel started receiving threats.

When I figured out about La Loba, that I had trespassed on her territory, I thought I could just apologize, maybe pay her the fee she would have received from the deal, and the whole thing would be forgotten. I passed a message through an intermediary and told her I was done with smuggling. I said it wasn't for me. But she wouldn't listen. I'm afraid she won't be satisfied until I'm dead."

"And you haven't called the police."

Tiff just looks at me. "No, I called you."

"There are no Venezuelans, are there?"

"La Loba may be Venezuelan. I don't know that she's not."

I open my mouth to ask Tiff what she thought I could have done with regard to La Loba, and then it hits me: the anonymous call, the convenient driver, the gun shop. . . .

"You lured me to that warehouse. You were the caller."

"I heard from a source that La Loba had chased a kill to Denver—a Thai-Canadian flesh peddler with legitimate businesses in cattle ranching. I knew she was going to be finishing him off over the weekend, so I arranged to have you watch."

"You hired me to kill her."

"In so many words."

"I told you, that's not what I do. I solve problems like cheating wives and runaway kids. I don't do hits."

"It wasn't going to be a hit. I'd been watching you for a while, Adcock. When I learned that you spent the winter in Denver with a woman, I saw an opportunity. I figured if I could make you think La Loba killed your girlfriend you might take her down."

"I don't understand. You thought I'd just assume La Loba was a threat to Connie?"

I stop.

"You hung the doll in Connie's apartment."

Tiff reaches out to touch my shoulder. "I'm sorry. . . ."

I slap her hand away. "Are you insane?"

"I realize now that getting your girlfriend involved was a mistake."

"A mistake! This is way more than a mistake. How would you feel if you came home and discovered that you'd been hanged in effigy?"

"She never saw it. She left town before I staged the scene."

"Where is she?"

"I went to the library on Saturday morning and told her that I was a friend of yours, that we were working on a case together, but the case had taken a bad turn and now her life was at risk. I gave her a plane ticket to San Francisco."

I pull out my phone and dial Connie's number. As usual, it goes to voice mail.

Tiff says, "I told her not to contact you or take your calls, in case the lines were tapped."

"Give me your phone."

Tiff goes to the living room and comes back with her purse. She produces an iPhone in a clear plastic case, unlocks the screen, and hands it to me. I dial Connie.

She doesn't answer.

"Where the hell is she, Tiff?"

"I haven't heard from her since she left town. I told her the danger would end when the Bay Dogs left Denver, so I bet you'll hear from her soon." She pauses. "I should never have let her believe she was in danger. That was wrong, and I'm sorry."

"You vandalized a woman's apartment in the most horrific way, after lying to her about your association with me. How many felonies is that? And by the way, if I were a member of the Denver police, I'd want to ask you some questions about Erik Magnusson. You know he was hanged?"

Her eyes go wide. "I had nothing to do with that."

"Who did it, then?"

"I have no idea."

For some reason, I believe her. Her eyes are as transparent and guileless as her blow-up doll's. I don't hate her, even though I should.

"I need your help, Johnny. I've been living in my plane for months. I don't know what to do!"

"Get out of my home."

When she's gone, I stare at the wall for a few minutes. I've had some disturbing cases over the years. I've watched wives fool around with my clients' best friends behind their backs; I've had clients' children deprogrammed from free-love cults. I've never had anything like this. My client just showed up at my door dressed like my girlfriend—who is currently incommunicado but was recently hanged in effigy by my client. It sounds like the setup for a joke. I wish I found it funny.

I sit down in the kitchen and go through my mail; the building's concierge brings it up while I'm on the road. Behind a shrink-wrapped stack of home-renovation catalogues I find a package half the size of a shoebox. The return address typed onto the UPS label is Connie's. Without thought to the contents—which should tell you something about my frame of mind—I slice the packing tape with a key. Inside, I find not a bomb or a packet of anthrax but a bottle of wine, a 2012 Zinfandel from a Sonoma County winery called Domaine Amphora. It looks expensive, but I'm no expert. Connie grew up in Sonoma, and many of her friends' parents worked in the wine industry. Now those same classmates run the family vineyards, and they occasionally send Connie bottles as gifts. I've had the pleasure of enjoying a few of them with her, but she's never sent any to me, and I'm not sure why she's starting now. I check the label on the box. It was sent the day before yesterday.

One of two things is happening here. Either Connie put this box in the mail before she went missing, or I'm looking at phase two of Tiff Tate's psychological campaign. It seems unlikely that Connie would have rushed out to mail me a bottle of wine on Friday, when we were going to meet for dinner the same night. Maybe she was planning ahead, a little present to greet me when I got home? It doesn't make sense—but neither does Tiff's sending me a bottle of wine to go with my blow-up doll.

I grab a corkscrew from a kitchen drawer, open the bottle, and pour a splash into a wineglass. It smells humid, earthy. I take a sip, then a gulp, and then another, waiting for the poison to hit. Three glasses in, I'm still not dead. Instead, I feel light-headed and a bit reckless. Drunk, I believe they call it. I take out my phone and scroll down to Izzy's number, but I stop before I tap her name. What kind of example would this set, drunk-dialing my daughter? I think about calling Connie again, but what's the point? She has received twenty messages from me over the last couple of days. She gets the idea.

I put my chin on the counter and stare at the bottle of wine. On the label, a craggy live-oak tree obscures a Spanish-style villa. Rows of grapevines fan out in front of the house like perspective lines. Tomorrow is a scheduled off-day. Looks like I'll be doing a little wine tasting?

# 23

Next morning, I'm on the road by seven, flying up the 101 in the lane reserved for carpools, electric cars, and idiots like me. The air is still cool, but the haze over the bay suggests it's going to be hot by afternoon. In Santa Clara, I see the light towers of the 49ers' new billion-dollar stadium. The price tag on that place still amazes me. A pro football team plays only eight regular season home games a year. Even if the Niners rent the place out once a month for concerts and maybe host an exhibition soccer match or two during the off season, you're still looking at three hundred nights a year on which no beer is poured, no T-shirts are sold, no parking fees collected. I'm sure there's a reason the NFL is the highest-grossing league in the world, but it can't be gate revenue.

Forty minutes later, I'm weaving through the streets of San Francisco. Here's a better use for a billion dollars: bore a tunnel under San Francisco. The city is surrounded on three sides by water, and there's still no freeway cutting through it, which means the only route from the southern suburbs to the northern ones is a long, slow crawl through miles of traffic lights. Block after block of all-night diners, Maserati dealers, and dildo shops. I know a freeway tunnel doesn't quicken the pulse like a new football stadium, but I guarantee it would get more use.

It's a little after nine when I reach Healdsburg, a sun-bleached town at the mouth of Dry Creek Valley. Like a lot of wine-country communities, Healdsburg caters to tourists seeking both expensive alcoholic beverages and rabbit-themed home accents. Connie says that Healdsburg was a different place when she was young, more Rockwell than Rockefeller, and that in some parts of town you could even find vandalism and poverty. That may have been true at one time, but, looking down the row of artisanal yarn shops and farm-to-table restaurants selling thirty-dollar chicken breasts, all I can think is that we're a long, long way from Baltimore.

The O'Connell home is on a leafy street a few blocks from the town square. It's a two-story Craftsman bungalow with squared-off pillars and a porch swing. I'm ashamed to admit that, even though I live in the same metropolitan area, this is my first time here.

I leave the bike a block from the house and walk the rest of the way. I am arriving unannounced by design—on cats' paws, as my grandma liked to say. I pause on the porch, listening to the voices in the living room, watching the shadows behind the curtains. I thought by the time I got here I'd know how to feel, but I don't. There is only one way Connie's disappearance makes sense, and I've been unable to get my head around it. Or maybe just unwilling.

I knock. Connie opens the door in a navy-blue terrycloth robe. Her dark hair is still wet from the shower. She holds a coffee mug in one hand. When she sees that it's me, she transfers the mug to the other hand and pushes open the screen door.

"Come in," she says calmly.

I don't, at first. I just stand there like the fool I have proven myself to be as she turns around and tells her father—he must be in the kitchen—"It's okay, I'm fine. Could you leave us alone for a minute?"

Returning to me, she asks if I've eaten breakfast. "I made some hard-boiled eggs."

"I'm not hungry," I say.

She nods as if that's what she expected. "Have a seat. I'll be right back. I should be dressed for this."

I lower myself into a wooden wing chair. Connie disappears soundlessly down the hall. The living room is filled with dark wood furniture in the Arts and Crafts style. The bookcases are full but not overfilled. No books sit horizontally on top of the rows; no stacks of magazines lie errant on the end tables. Everything is in its place. I can see where Connie gets her professional inspiration.

*I should be dressed for this.* In my head I compare Connie's prudent instinct to match her attire to the occasion with Tiff Tate's choice of attire for difficult conversations. Then again, maybe Tiff is only protecting herself. When you're naked, there's no way to get caught with your pants down.

A moment later, Connie returns, dressed in tight-fitting jeans and a sleeveless linen top. Her hair is twisted up. She's wearing no makeup.

"I wanted to call you," she says. "You deserve an explanation."

"Is it because I'm a ballplayer?"

"I never had a problem with that. My dad had concerns, but not me. I was fine with all of it: the hours, the travel, even the other women."

"About that, listen. . . ."

"Let me finish. It wasn't the baseball life that scared me, John, it was your other career. I never agreed to date a private eye."

"I was always honest with you about what I did in my spare time."

"You told me, that's true. And I thought I understood what it might mean for me—a little more travel in the off season, maybe. You made it sound so benign, like you just . . . not rescued kittens from trees, but something along those lines. You helped your friends solve problems that required discretion. And that was fine with me. I think we all could use a friend like that. But you weren't being completely honest."

"Had I known this was going to happen, this mess with Tiff Tate, I would never have taken the case. She misled me. I thought I was just going to speak with some players, ask some questions. Nothing like this."

"John, I have thought about this for hours. Days. More than you can imagine. I suppose it's possible that you didn't know, but I'm sorry, I just don't believe it. When we saw the couple in the restaurant, you could have explained what was going on."

"I didn't know! I honestly didn't know who she was, or who was pulling his strings. Would you believe Tiff, of all people, smuggled him out of Cuba?"

"At the very least, you knew the situation was more opaque than you originally thought. I mean, he wouldn't talk to you. Didn't that strike you as odd?"

"Of course, but it was my problem, not yours. I wanted to keep you out of it."

"Well, you failed."

"I know."

"And I just can't have that in my life. I don't need to be hunted."

"It wasn't true! That was just a story Tiff told you."

"It doesn't matter. You led me there like a lamb to the slaughter. Is that how you tried to keep me out of it?"

I look at my shoes. "I swear I didn't know."

"And that's not even what really bothered me. What concerned me was that if I stayed with you this was going to be my life. Let's suppose I wasn't in danger this time. What about the next case? You weren't going to retire. How many times did you tell me this was your retirement plan, the next direction in your life, the thing that was going to keep you from selling insurance or real estate for the rest of your life? This wasn't a one-time deal. This was going to be a constant thing, a constant threat. I don't know, maybe your other girlfriends like it that way. Maybe they like to have their lives threatened, but I can tell you I do not. Once is too much for me. Do you understand?"

She pauses, waiting for me to reply, but I have nothing to say. She's right about all of it.

"I'm sorry for leaving the way I did. I was so frightened, I didn't know who to trust."

"Does your father know why you left?"

"He knows everything. We are completely honest with each other."

This hurts, but I absorb it. "I'm sorry, Connie. I never meant to put you in this situation. You're safe now."

"It's too late, John. I'm done."

"Done with what? With me?"

"Yes, with you."

"But here's the thing: I'm going to quit. I should have quit before all this happened, but now I'm going to do it."

"You sound like an alcoholic. Please don't quit on my account. If the investigations make you happy, you shouldn't stop doing them. You're not going to play baseball forever, and I understand that you need something to take its place. Maybe it's this, maybe not. I wish you well either way."

"I don't want your well wishes, I want you. Let's erase last weekend. Can we do that? Let's go back to where we were in the off season: a fire in your apartment, singers on the stereo. Remember?"

"How could I forget? But that's over."

In the silence, I gather my thoughts. Yesterday I feared she was dead. Now she's alive, but she wants nothing to do with me. This is why I've been single so long. This is the risk of commitment, right here. "When are you going back to Denver?"

"I'm not going back. I don't feel safe there."

"But your whole life is in Denver."

She shrugs. "It was."

This hits me like a punch in the chest. Not only have I ruined a perfectly good relationship, I've also ruined Connie's life. Here she is, over thirty, unemployed, living in her father's house. Through conversations about her work, I've come to know that jobs in her field are few and far between. She always said she was lucky to have that position at the Denver Public Library—a statement I thought was false modesty, but now I see that her job was sort of like mine. Denver Public isn't the Yankees, but it is the Rockies. I get that now.

Connie wipes her eyes and puts her arms around my neck. For a moment I indulge the hope that she will change her mind, but something has changed between us. I have broken her trust, and for Connie that is irreparable. She pulls me tight. By the time her tears soak through my shirt, I know it's over. "Goodbye, John," she whispers.

# 24

The Dry Creek Valley road is sticky under the wheels of my bike, thanks to the scorching sun and a recent coat of asphalt. I'm sweating under my helmet and leathers. A couple miles into the valley, the new asphalt ends, and the road goes back to its old shitty self. The smells change, too: petrochemical stink gives way to the anise of the scrub brush and the astringent mint of the eucalyptus trees. Neat rows of grapevines stretch across the valley floor and up the opposite slope. I'm impressed by how rustic the scenery becomes just a few miles out of town. Shingles on mailboxes announce tasting rooms, but when I look down the driveways all I see is farm equipment, tumbleweeds, and roosters. Scrawny goats graze barnyards of dry grass. Out past the new asphalt, this is no country for tour buses.

After seven winding miles, I arrive at the address on the bottle. A wooden sign nailed to the trunk of a live oak announces *Domaine Amphora* in the same typeface as the label. I leave my bike behind a smoke bush. On foot I feel smart and alive, like I'm running into the game from the bullpen. I have to remind myself this is no game. If I get too aggressive here, there's no catcher to cool me off with a visit to the mound, no pitching coach to tap my ass and tell me he loves me. This is me risking my life. I'm not sure what I expect to find at the top of the driveway. It could be a hooded guard with a Kalashnikov, or a retired banker pouring tastes of his estate Cabernet. Neither sounds like much fun.

After a couple of doglegs, the driveway opens into a parking lot fringed with dusty rosemary and lavender. There is only one car in the lot, an old diesel Mercedes with California plates. The sedan has a bumper sticker that reads SAVE WATER—DRINK SONOMA WINE. Bumper stickers are a strange phenomenon. Most people would rather tattoo their skin than put a sticker on their car. Nearly all of my teammates have ink, but you won't find a single sticker in the players' parking lot. I walk around the car to a ranch house that serves as Domaine Amphora's tasting room. A sign on the door states the hours and age restrictions, along with some bullshit about dogs being welcome as long as they're over three. The sign is made of wood cut into the shape of a handled jar. An amphora, I read on the winery's website, is a kind of jar used in ancient Greece to transport olive oil and other marketable liquids. Turns out I knew this already from an in-flight magazine I read years ago, an issue dedicated to "the new Greece" (aka Turkey), where apparently you can scuba-dive to the wrecks of ancient container ships filled with two-thousand-year-old jars. Some of them still have wine in them.

I stride to the door, my boot heels knocking on the wooden porch, and discover that it's locked. I step back and check the hours. They should be open. Guess I'm not the only one playing hooky on this Monday afternoon. I pull out my phone and call the tasting room's number. I hear a phone ring inside the house, but no one answers. Now I'm irritated. I didn't come all this way just to get dumped. This was supposed to be my chance to make something of the day.

From the far end of the porch, I see that there are more buildings behind the house. Tall, windowless structures with enormous sliding doors. Barns. Connie said the wine business is really about logistics: storing wine in barrels, then in bottles, then moving bottles to market. The actual winemaking—crushing grapes, blending juice—takes a couple of days. The rest is waiting. And paying rent.

I step off the porch and walk toward the warehouses. Something tells me it's a good idea to announce myself, just in case the owner of the Mercedes turns out to be an armed guard.

"Hello! Anybody here? Any chance I could taste some wine?"

No answer.

I approach the first barn. The sliding door, ten feet tall and almost as wide, is open six inches or so. I lift my sunglasses and peer inside. Wooden barrels are stacked on steel racks from floor to ceiling, occupying every cubic yard of space inside the building. It reminds me of IKEA, but much more dense. I understand now why the doors are so large, and why they're installed on two sides of the barn. If you needed a barrel in the far corner, you'd be better off removing the wall than trying to get there from here.

"Anybody in here? Hello?"

*Don't bother us,* the barrels say, *we're aging.*

The second barn is a bit smaller than the first, both shorter and narrower, and the weathered siding suggests that it's older as well. The sliding doors are rusty. I can't budge the near one, so I move around to the back door, which is already open. I duck inside and remove my shades. Instead of barrels, this building is filled with winemaking equipment: hoses and screw presses and enormous stainless-steel tanks.

Then I see why no one answered the phone. A man in a winery-branded polo shirt dangles from a steel fermentation tank, a pink nylon rope knotted expertly around his neck. His head lolls lifelessly to one side, dead eyes staring. I take several steps backward. My shoulder collides with something in the

140

darkness. I spin around. It's a white athletic shoe, attached to a meaty leg. Hanging from the tank behind me is a woman in an identical polo shirt. She's white, middle-aged. A double suicide? The pink rope suggests otherwise. There were identical nylon fibers on the beam in Magnusson's video room.

I know I should call the police, but what good will that do? These two aren't going to benefit from medical attention. The one who needs help is me. This is a setup. And it may already be too late.

I run through the yellow grass around the barns, toward the main house. If the killer is here, if he's watching me, then he has probably moved my bike. And if the bike is gone—then what? What am I going to do? What kind of idiot rides out here alone, unarmed, on an anonymous tip? I feel like a chump.

When I reach the parking lot, I fall into the trap—but it's not the trap I imagined. Two police cruisers from the Sonoma County Sheriff's Department are idling behind the Mercedes with their light bars flashing. When the officers see me, they leap out of their cars and crouch behind the doors, just like they do on TV. They draw their weapons.

"Stop where you are!" yells one of the cops. His head is cocked sideways, staring down the barrel of his nine-millimeter pistol. "Don't move! Put your hands where we can see them and get down on the ground!"

"Do it now!" yells his partner, crouched behind the passenger's door of the same car. "Get down now!"

I do as they say, first kneeling in the dirt, and then lying facedown with my hands clasped behind my head. When the deputy comes to frisk me, he smells like cheap shampoo-conditioner mix, the kind they load into the dispensers in minor-league clubhouses. He pats my flanks and crotch with his hands, then yells back to his colleagues, "He's clean!"

His partner plus the two cops from the other cruiser stumble over, belts a-jingling. "We got a call about someone screaming," one of them says above me. I turn my head to the side and look up. The cop's body is blocking the sun. "Know anything about that?"

"I just got here."

"Looks like you were in a hurry to leave."

"I came to taste wine, but the door was locked, so I looked around."

"Find anything we should know about?"

I realize there's no point being coy. "Look in the second barn, the low one. There are two stiffs inside. That's why I was running. It scared the shit out of me."

I hear the clink of gear and dusty footfalls as two cops peel off to investigate. The sergeant gets on his radio, reporting an incident with possible fatalities. "We're gonna need forensics," he says. The radio squelches in his earpiece. "What's that? No, I don't think so. Suspect is in custody."

A few minutes later, the deputy returns. "Sergeant, we found two victims, male and female, both Caucasian. Looks like suicide by hanging."

"It wasn't suicide," I say.

Both cops look down. The sergeant says, "You do realize it's better for you to stay quiet."

"Just trying to help."

"You should be helping yourself, is what you should be doing."

Second time this week I've gotten that advice.

"He's right," the deputy adds. "We give you the right to remain silent. You should take it."

For some reason, that does it. Not staring down two drawn weapons, not finding myself facedown in the dust, not even being called "the suspect." No, it isn't until I have cops feeling sorry for me—giving me advice about how to act in my own self-interest—that I realize I'm in the shit. And deep.

# 25

The interrogation room of the Sonoma County Sheriff's Department is air-conditioned to three degrees below freezing. The detective in the chair across from me wears long sleeves, a tie, and a jacket. He's a middle-aged Latino, clean-shaven and only a little overweight. He's been reasonable so far, but these guys work in teams. Soon the bell will ring and they'll send in the Bad Cop.

"Tell me again why you were on the Domaine Amphora property."

"I was there to taste wine."

"So it was a pleasure trip."

"That's right."

"And what kind of work do you do?"

I pause. Usually, this is my trump card. Over the years, my answer to this question has scored me everything from free drinks to airline upgrades, even a few private tours behind police tape. This time, however, it feels like a liability. "I'm a professional baseball player."

The detective raises his brow. "Oh, really? Anybody I've heard of?"

"I'm a reliever for the Bay Dogs." He already knows my name.

"Oh, sure. San José, right?" The detective steals a glance at the clock on the wall. It's a little after four. "Guess you're gonna miss tonight's game."

"We're off today. That's why I went wine tasting." I'm trying hard to keep the irritation out of my voice, but it's tough.

"Right, right." He taps his pencil on his notebook. "Wait here a sec?"

Ten minutes later he's back. "You sure you don't want to call a lawyer?"

"Am I under arrest?"

"No, but if there were charges brought against you, everything you say to us could be used in court."

"I understand my rights."

"Mr. Adcock, you seem like a reasonably smart guy. Think about this from my perspective. We get a report of, quote, bloodcurdling screams coming from a vineyard, and when officers arrive, they find you running from the scene. It doesn't look good for you."

I say nothing.

"We find your motorcycle hidden in the bushes near the road—presumably that's where you were headed when the officers apprehended you." He sighs. "I don't want to arrest you, but what choice do I have? Do yourself a favor and call someone."

I consider my options. Connie is the only person I know in Sonoma County, and I can't call her. Not like this. I have some pride left.

No, I just need to wait this out. It's only a matter of time before the police connect this murder with the Magnusson case. I've already told them to call the Denver PD. You'd have to be an idiot not to see the similarities. Not only the hanging, but the type of rope. And what else? Oh, right: if they look closely, they'll find that the same man was in the vicinity both times.

That being me.

Fine, I need a lawyer. But who? Todd Ratkiss went to law school. . . . Maybe he could make a referral? Then I remember my clubhouse keycard.

"Where's the phone?" I ask the detective.

He smiles, pleased that I've finally come to my senses. "Do you know the number?"

"It's in my wallet."

"No problem, hold on." He knocks to be let out and returns a minute later with my wallet and a cordless phone. I'm surprised this is how it goes; I thought police-station calls were made at a pay phone in a dingy concrete cell where you have to blow your cellmate for a dime.

I pull out my keycard and dial the 800 number on the back. A woman answers on the first ring. "MLB Helpline, Janet speaking."

"This is Johnny Adcock of the Bay Dogs. Can I speak to Feldspar, please?"

"Mr. Feldspar is traveling this afternoon. May I take a message?"

A message? This was supposed to be like 911. "Tell him I've been arrested, or I'm about to be."

Without a hint of panic, Janet asks, "Where are you right now, Mr. Adcock?"

"The sheriff's station in Sonoma County."

I hear typing. "Is that the headquarters in Santa Rosa or one of the field offices?"

"Santa Rosa."

"Okay, Santa Rosa . . . and what are the charges?"

"Murder, I think. But it's bullshit." I meet eyes with the detective, who looks away. "I mean, I'm innocent. But I need a lawyer."

More typing. "We'll let Mr. Feldspar make that determination. I assume we can reach you at this number?"

"How long until Feldspar calls me back?"

"He's usually very prompt. Just sit tight, Mr. Adcock. Help is on the way."

We hang up, and I feel surprisingly confident. *Help is on the way?* You'd think I called the Avengers.

The detective gathers up the phone and my wallet. "I have a sheet of local attorneys, if you need them."

"I thought I only got one call."

The detective waggles his hand. "Give or take," he says.

I am considering taking him up on the offer when the phone rings. The detective answers, and I hear a man's voice light into him. I can't make out exactly what the caller is saying, but he's pissed.

Then the detective hands me the phone. "He wants to speak with you."

"Hello?"

"Adcock, it's Feldspar. From now on, your mouth doesn't work. Understand?"

"Yes."

"I'll be there soon." The line goes dead.

The detective and I are both a little stunned. I hand back the phone and he asks if I'd like a cup of coffee.

I start to say, "Yes, I would," but stop myself. I give a thumbs-up instead.

# 26

The detective tells me it will be tomorrow at the earliest before I get my bike back. It's already on a truck headed for the impound lot in Petaluma.

"Okay," I say. "I'll come up tomorrow morning."

"Actually"—he looks cautiously at Feldspar—"we can have it delivered. What's your address?"

Twenty minutes later, I'm in the passenger's seat of Jim Feldspar's rented SUV, heading south on 101. For most of the ride, Feldspar has been listening to his messages one by one through the Bluetooth in his ear, then calling his assistant to give instructions on matters I lack the context to understand. Finally, when it appears he has reached the end of his task list, I jump in. "You have to tell me what you did back there," I say. I'm not flattering him; it was a remarkable performance. He showed up and went into the chief's office, and five minutes later I was signing for my wallet, keys, and phone. No charges filed, no further questions asked.

Feldspar's brow rises. "When Janet told me you were in Sonoma, I figured it was fifty-fifty you'd be released by sundown. I know lots of people in Sonoma. This part of the country was the Eagle's power base."

"The Eagle?"

For the briefest moment he takes his eyes off the road and looks at me. "President Clinton. We were in California once a quarter at least, and more often than that during election season. Lots of money out here."

"So you met the sheriff through the president?"

"Secret Service has what are called advance teams, groups of agents who travel ahead, making preparations for the visit. So, if the Eagle was doing a fund-raiser in Santa Rosa, for instance, one of us had to meet with Santa Rosa PD and Sonoma Sheriff to plan for street closures, helipad access, rooftop security along the motorcade route, that type of thing. It's a million little details you have to think about, but after a while it becomes routine."

"And along the way you meet a lot of cops."

"After the business is taken care of, you find yourself in a Holiday Inn in a town you don't know." He pauses. "It's sort of like baseball. You end up hitting the same towns year after year, and you get to be friends with the local guys. That guy Vasquez, in the sheriff's office—"

"The detective?"

He shakes his head. "His boss. When I met him he was a beat officer. He took me to a cowboy bar in Petaluma, sawdust on the floor, the whole bit. People were line-dancing in boots and heels. I walk up to the bar to buy the first pitcher, and Vasquez taps me on the shoulder and he says, 'Not here. Come with me.' And he takes me to the back of the room, past the restrooms, where he stands in front of this unmarked door and knocks some kind of secret code. The door opens up, and I'm staring into this other room, very dark, with a different kind of music. Topless girls everywhere, you know. This waitress walks right up and greets Vasquez by name, asking where he's been. . . ."

Feldspar stares out the window, where the Marin tower of the Golden Gate Bridge rises above the hills. "Anyway, when Janet said Sonoma Sheriff, I said a little prayer that Jack Vasquez was still on the force. Then I called, and it turned out he was the supervisor in charge of your case. Right then the odds went from even to near a hundred percent." He drums the steering wheel with his thumbs. "Until that point, though, there were no guarantees."

"So you just asked your friend to let me walk?" I try not to sound incredulous, but I really can't believe this is how it works. I always suspected as much, and I'm glad to be free, but I feel like my view of the criminal-justice system will never be the same.

"It wasn't that straightforward," Feldspar says. "I couldn't ask him to turn you loose for no reason."

"What reason did you give?"

"It wasn't hard to fix up. He knows you didn't do it."

"You convinced him?"

"Me? I didn't have to convince him. You told him you were tasting wine, and he believed you. Also, forensics determined the time of death was at least three hours before you arrived. That was good for you. I just pushed a little, that's all. My job is to protect ballplayers. Now, do I believe that you were tasting wine? It just so happens that I do not."

"But that's not your job."

Feldspar looks at me. "Incorrect. My job is to protect you, and if you're going to continue to place yourself in situations where you end up arrested or in jail, then it is very much my business to uncover your lies. And I will uncover them, Adcock. Make no frickin' mistake about that."

The tenor of the conversation has changed just as quickly as the landscape: we are now skirting the misty hills of Tiburon, carving our way down to the bridge. The rental car goes dark as we plow into a tunnel.

"You got lucky this time," Feldspar says. "If I hadn't once witnessed Jack Vasquez slipping his fingers into a stripper's thong, you might be on the front page of tomorrow's paper. Lead story on *SportsCenter*, a disgrace to the sport, et cetera et cetera. Guilty or not, it doesn't matter—your career would be over. And you know what? Nobody in baseball would give a shit. You're nothing, Adcock. Kids don't buy tickets to see you. The game would go on, remember that."

"Hold on," I protest, "I went for a ride in the country on my day off, and you assume I'm acting out?"

"Save your breath. That part of our conversation is over. I think I've made it clear what will happen if we catch you working a case. And, really, what are you hoping to accomplish, anyway? You get paid over a million bucks a year to throw a ball. Leave the crime fighting to the authorities. Do you know how many cops would quit their jobs to have your life? Assholes like you make me crazy. You don't realize what you have."

Did this rental car come with a soapbox?

"Same thing with these jackasses selling cars or whatever on TV. . . . When I was playing ball, guys like George Brett and Jim Palmer did commercials because the pay was low, relatively speaking, and they knew their shelf life was limited. Nowadays, you all make so much in salary that it's obvious when someone's doing an endorsement out of greed."

Now and then you find yourself in a situation like this. The union advises players never to talk about their contracts, and this is one of the reasons why. The best strategy is to say nothing. It's your right to remain silent, after all.

"Maybe you've heard this story," Feldspar says. "Do you remember Marvin Miller? You probably don't. He was the head of the players' association back in the day. Well, Miller was standing around the batting cage one day in San Francisco, and he said to the guy he was with, 'You see Bobby Bonds over there? I'll bet you one day that his son makes more money in a single season than Willie Mays has made in his career.' And you know what? Turns out he was wrong! Turns out Barry Bonds made more in one year than the *entire freaking Giants team* made in their careers. And you're saying that, on top of that, you need to sell me a car? It's disgusting. . . ."

Of course, I'm not saying anything of the sort. No car companies are knocking on my door. In fact, my value to a brand may be less than zero. I recently had the displeasure to discover that in the Bay Dogs' stadium shop a baseball autographed by me sells for less than an unsigned ball. But I let Feldspar finish his rant. I understand why he feels this way. I'd say the same things if I were in his shoes.

"Times have changed," I say.

"You got that right."

"And about the other thing, don't worry. I'm done with investigations. From here on, it's just baseball."

"We'll see, Adcock."

"Thanks for saving my ass. You know, it's amazing what you've done, bridging careers and all."

"What do you say we cut the bullshit?"

"Excuse me? I was trying to pay a compliment."

"Let me remind you that I put you on your ass once, and I'm trained, willing, and ready to do it again if need be."

"Hey, now—"

"Now that we have some time to talk, why don't you tell me what you know about the Magnusson case?"

The SUV rumbles onto the bridge deck. Beside the roadway, tourists lean on cruiser bikes, taking in the view of Alcatraz. The San Francisco skyline sparkles in the distance, the bay spread out before it like a shark-infested welcome mat.

"I know he was a friend of yours."

"Is it against the law to have friends?"

"You sound like my teenage son. Murder always has a reason, Adcock. Do your friend a favor. Help me figure out why he was killed."

So the cops have determined he was murdered. I should feel vindicated, but I don't.

"I'd tell you why if I knew."

"I'm sure you would. I'm just asking for your help. What if I told you that Yonel Ruiz lived with Erik Magnusson for a month last winter?"

"A month? He said it was only a week."

"So you two talked about Ruiz?"

"Only once, briefly."

"And what did he say?"

"Just that Ruiz stayed with him before he got his own place."

"How did that go?"

"Fine."

"No arguments, fights?"

"He didn't mention any."

"So he didn't say anything about Ruiz that would make you want to peg him in the back with a fastball?" Before I can answer, Feldspar looks me in the eye and says, "We both know the ball didn't slip. And there's no need to keep lying about it. You served your suspension—the case is closed. So you might as well be honest."

"I had my reasons." There's more I could tell him—about my batting-practice conversation with Ruiz, about Tiff Tate, about La Loba—and some of it may be useful to him, who knows? But to tell him any of it would involve admitting that I'm still working the detective beat. He's been very clear about the consequences there.

"Was it just your typical beef?" Feldspar suggests. "Remember, I was a pitcher once. I know the deal. It could have been that someone on the Rockies threw at one of your guys the day before. It could have been payback for a home run earlier in the game, I don't know. But you have to admit, the coincidence is—what's the word—conspicuous? Your friend Erik Magnusson is killed in his office, and the next afternoon you plunk Ruiz, who happened to live with Magnusson when he was fresh off the boat."

"Like you said, it's a coincidence."

Feldspar exhales dramatically as he accelerates through the FasTrak toll gate. "You think I'm an idiot, don't you?" He pauses. "Don't say anything; I know the answer. I would probably think the same thing if I were you. Here's this cop—because that's what I am to you, right? And you're not wrong, in a way. Here's this cop who wants to spoil my fun. So why should I speak to him? What has he ever done for me?"

"I thanked you, Feldspar. I appreciate what you did up there."

"I know you do. But I think you're wrong about me. You and me, we're not that different. I'm working to protect the game of baseball, the institution of baseball, this game we all love and cherish. I don't know for sure, but I have a hunch you're doing the same thing. I mean, why would you risk life and limb to chase some dead player's wife to Tijuana? You don't even bill your clients. It's a labor of love, Adcock. I know what you're doing, because I'm doing the same thing."

"I assume you get paid."

"I do, but it's a fraction of what I could make in another position. Do you know how much ex–Secret Service guys can pull down as private security consultants? I have a friend who went to Abu Dhabi—do you know where that is?"

"I get it. You're one of the good guys."

"I know stuff you don't know," he says. "Through my network, through my position, I have access to information you don't have. About Magnusson. About Ruiz. You don't have to say anything. I'm done asking questions. But if you want to talk, you know how to reach me."

# 27

Feldspar leaves me in front of my building. I'm surprised how calm I feel, given the events of the day, until I find myself alone in the elevator and my nerves start releasing what they've been holding back. I start to sweat. I keep thinking of those bodies hanging from the wine tanks—a middle-aged man and his wife, the detectives informed us, not the owners of the vineyard but a couple of retired teachers who worked part-time in the tasting room.

Maybe Feldspar is right. Maybe I should turn this one over to him and his buddies. I wouldn't want a police detective pitching the eighth inning—what makes me think I can do their job?

In a word: arrogance. Which isn't necessarily a negative in sports. Without arrogance, how does someone like me think he can slip a ball past a monster like Yonel Ruiz? I heard an interview with a novelist who claimed that all writers are ego-maniacs. Who else, he argued, believes that what he has to say is so important that it should be printed on millions of dead trees and sold for $26.95 per copy? Pitchers think that way, too. When a guy walks up to the plate with a bat on his shoulder, we think: Fuck that, I'll show him who owns the zone. It's infantile, but it's never going to change. Ballplayers are babies, and everyone knows you can't reason with a baby.

My phone ran out of juice in Sonoma. I wasn't able to check my messages during the long ride home with Feldspar. When I finally plug in, I see a missed call from Briggman at the Marriott and another from Anibal Martín. It's too late to call Cuba, so I dial Salt Lake. Briggman answers on the first ring.

"Adcock, I found your lady." He laughs. "You didn't tell me about the hair!"

Imagine a senior citizen with the hairstyle of a 1960s Bond girl, dyed coal black and teased from the roots. That's Kitty Marlborough, and, despite the ghastly appearance, she's a pleasure to be around, kind and soft-spoken with a laugh that comes easily and often. At charity dinners she is always the first wife to welcome the parents of the cancer-stricken child, the disaster survivors, the widows of the fallen marines. I never would have pegged her for an adulteress. Maybe she's not. Maybe this will be the exception that proves the rule.

"I'm going to send you a clip. Hold on a sec. . . ." I hear rustling on Briggman's end, and then my phone vibrates with a new message. On the screen I see a grainy video frame. I press play.

We are in a hotel conference room, looking over ten or fifteen rows of spectators toward a dais where the presenter stands at a podium. The unmistakable bouffant of Kitty Marlborough looms behind the microphone. Some kind of digital filter has been applied so that Kitty's head appears brighter, like there's a spotlight trained on her face. She is smiling, gesturing with both hands as she speaks. She's wearing business attire, a double-breasted suit over a light-colored blouse. Next to the podium, an older man sits at a table. Behind them, a projector screen displays some kind of map. The security camera must be located somewhere high on the rear wall, or maybe in the ceiling, because we're watching this from high above.

"Is there sound?" I ask.

"Just watch," Briggman says.

Kitty finishes her presentation—or I gather that she finishes, because the map disappears and she walks away from the podium. The man at the table stands up. They shake hands. He leads the audience in a round of applause.

"It's neat what OmniSentry is trying to do with this system," Briggman says. "They're addressing the problem we have in the security industry of too many cameras and not enough time. You can cover every square foot of a property with cameras, but someone needs to watch the footage if you're going to get any value out of it. OmniSentry does all that for you. You upload a couple photos of someone, and it creates a mathematical fingerprint of that person's face, then searches all the footage and cuts together a montage. Or you can just watch in real time, following the person through the facility. It's kind of brilliant."

"Is it?"

"I think so, but I'm twisted."

Cut to another camera, this one a view of a lobby carpeted in a wide geometrical pattern, elevators in the distance. Well-dressed men and women drift into the frame from the right. Briggman's software highlights Kitty's face in the crowd. She is shaking hands and smiling—working the room, as I've seen her do so many times.

Another cut and we're in a hallway; this picture is grainier than the last two, and, unlike the others, it is only black and white. We watch the empty hall for a few seconds, and then Kitty's hair rises quickly from the bottom of the frame. She's walking down the hall, away from the camera.

Cut again and we're seeing the same hall from another angle.

It's a floor of guest rooms—there are numbers and card readers on the doors. Kitty stops before one of the doors and taps a card to the reader. She opens the door and disappears inside.

"Tell me what's happening," Briggman says.

"She just went into a hotel room."

He snorts, but before I can ask him what's so funny, the door opens again. Out walks a different woman, a housekeeper in a knee-length uniform skirt with a kerchief tied around her head. I check the timecode at the bottom right. Ten minutes have elapsed since we saw Kitty go in.

"What just happened?" I ask Briggman. "Who's this maid?"

"Keep watching."

The housekeeper smooths down the front of her skirt and checks her apron tie. She leaves the frame.

Cut back to the lobby scene. The realtors are still mingling. Our housekeeper enters stage left, her head spotlighted by the software. She walks purposefully toward one of the realtors and taps him on the shoulder. I recognize him as the man from the dais. They exchange a few words, and he follows her out of the room.

Cut to the hall, the two of them walking side by side. Then a shot before a hotel-room door. It's the same room, same number as before. The maid waits patiently while the man finds his key and taps it to the reader. He holds the door open for her, and she takes a step, but before she can slip inside, he seizes her in his arms and kisses her neck passionately. Her head rolls back with pleasure, and I see her face clearly.

"Jesus, it's Kitty."

"That's another great thing about OmniSentry," Briggman says. "You can't fool the algorithm. A suspect can be disguised, and the system will still pick him out. Or her, as the case may be."

Quick cut. Half an hour has elapsed. Door opens again, and

this time I see the man standing there in bathing trunks with a towel draped over his shoulder. He scratches his saggy old-man tits, looks at his watch, and leaves the frame.

Another cut, same camera, ten minutes later. Door opens, and there's Kitty Marlborough, back in her double-breasted suit. Her hair has been restored to its full architectural glory.

"What do you think?" Briggman asks when the video ends. "Should we buy this thing? It's expensive, but it's hard to argue with the results."

Something occurs to me. "Does it require special cameras?"

"No, it's all standard equipment. OmniSentry is really just signal-processing software."

"You said it works in real time as well."

"That's right."

"I wonder if it could work remotely. Like, could you direct camera feeds from somewhere else into the system?"

"Interesting question. I'll ask the rep." Briggman pauses. "Come to think of it, I'm sure they've thought of this use case. OmniSentry's parent company makes drones."

"You should ask them to throw one into the deal!"

"A drone?" Briggman laughs. "I'd love that. Not sure what my boss would think, though."

# 28

I call Don Anibal, the Bay Dogs' Cuban scout, first thing in the morning. It is 7:00 a.m. California time, but Cuba is three hours ahead, so I figure Don Anibal is either at the office or on his way there. The one and only time we've met in person, at the Bay Dogs' spring-training facility in Arizona, he told me that he works out of a trailer parked next to a municipal ball field in suburban Havana. I started to express outrage at the inadequate facilities—shouldn't the Bay Dogs provide him with a real office? He stopped me and explained that the trailer works better than a suite in some air-conditioned office building. "The players in Cuba," he said, "they feel better if you look like their uncle, if you act like their uncle. If you act too big, they feel threatened. Is better, this trailer, *más cubano*."

When Don Anibal picks up the phone, the ping of aluminum bats in the background summons a vivid scenario: teenage boys in ragtag uniforms running drills on a dusty diamond, while Uncle Anibal reclines in a beach chair outside his trailer like a retiree in a campground. Cigar in mouth, straw Panama hat on his greasy bald head, he looks like Hannibal Lecter at the end of *Silence of the Lambs*—a look he claims the boys find soothing.

*"How are you, sisterfucker?"* Remember those machine-gun

rants of Ricky Ricardo's on *I Love Lucy*? Cubans really speak that way, like their tongues are on fire. No time for trailing consonants.

"*Doing well, and you?*"

"*Not bad, not bad. Bet you are glad to be back from fucking Colorado, eh?*"

I don't know if he's referring to the case, the fact that we dropped two of three in Denver, or the general displeasure of pitching at five thousand feet. "*Yes, I'm glad to be home.*"

"*Eh, socio, I have some news for you about our friend Pascual Alcalá.*"

"*Oh yes? What did you learn?*"

Don Anibal laughs. "*Not a fucking thing. I could not find anyone by that name. No ballplayers, not even a fucking plumber! I looked everywhere—birth records, death records, even high-school baseball rosters. Nothing, nobody, nowhere.*"

"*Government records are bad in Cuba, no?*"

"*For births and deaths, that is correct, but for baseball—fuck me, that's a different story. Baseball is a very important priority for the party and everyone in power.*"

"*Because of Fidel?*"

"*You got it. He wanted to play professional ball, you know. So the records of the baseball championships are very accurate. Trust me, if your friend Alcalá had played ball on this island, I would have found his name.*"

"*Is it possible that someone could have altered the records and removed his name?*"

"*I suppose that could have happened, but I doubt it. Baseball records are kept in two places—the local municipality offices and at the party headquarters in La Habana.*"

"*They keep amateur baseball records at the party headquarters?*"

"*They say the records go directly to Fidel. He uses them to draft players for his fantasy team.*"

*"And you checked those records?"*

*"Hell, yes, I did! The name Anibal Martín may not mean anything to you, but it opens doors down here."*

In the background, a ball explodes off a metal bat, and boys whoop and holler.

*"Well, thanks for checking."*

*"It was my pleasure,"* he says, *"and, speaking of pleasure, have I told you about Raúl's new sucia?"*

I hang up.

Unless Yonel Ruiz has a connection with access to Fidel's cache of fantasy-baseball data—and the balls not only to examine those records but to alter them—then it looks like we've reached a dead end. Is it possible that Magnusson misspelled the name?

Five minutes with Ruiz, that's all I need. Problem is, if Alcalá is in fact a Fausto Carmona situation, he's not going to talk to me about it. After what I did last week, he likely won't talk to me at all—not that I have any way of reaching him.

I do, however, have a number for Ruiz's "sister." For obvious reasons, I have been hesitant to contact La Loba since the incident with the butcher saw, but what could it hurt at this point? Someone, possibly La Loba, tried to frame me for a double murder. I've broken the seal on risk.

Enriqueta answers my call with unexpected enthusiasm. *"Hello, Johnny! I thought you forgot about me!"*

*"Enriqueta, I will never forget you."*

*"You are sweet."*

*"Not as sweet as you."*

*"Ay señor, you haven't fallen in love with me, have you?"*

*"You say that like it's a bad thing!"*

*"Love is always bad, Johnny. It makes us ignore our good judgment."*

She's a murderer. She cuts her enemies into stew meat. I am

ignoring good judgment, but let's be clear: it's not because I'm in love.

"When can I see you?"

"Oh, Johnny, I am so busy right now."

"Come to San José."

"I cannot come to you," she says, suddenly stern. "Call someone else. I'm sure a ballplayer like you can find a girl."

"I don't want another girl. I want you."

"Are you listening to me? I said I can't come to San José!"

"What if I called Tiff Tate? If I could arrange a meeting for the three of us—you, me, and Tiff Tate—could you find time in your busy schedule?"

This gets a nibble. "What exactly are you proposing?"

"A social occasion," I say, "so you can get to know each other. You are interested in meeting her, right?"

"Very much, but why would she agree to meet me? I'm nothing, an immigrant girl, and she is a respected leader in her industry. It would be better, I think, if she does not know I am coming."

"What if I told her you were a hired girl?"

"A prostitute?"

"Yes, but a sophisticated one."

"She would like that?"

"I know she will. Then, after we become acquainted with one another, we can reveal that you are the sister of a ballplayer, that you admire her and have questions."

"She won't be offended by the trick?"

I laugh. "No, she will be delighted. Tiff likes to pretend."

"Very good," La Loba says. "Tell me when and where, and I will be there."

# 29

Next day I'm at the park by 10:00 a.m. to do my lifting. It's Tuesday—chest and lats. Because it's so early and there's no one around to spot me, I do my bench presses on a machine, dialing in slightly more weight than I'd put on a bar. The trainers tell us that the machines are the same, that they work your muscles just as well as free weights, but everyone knows that's bullshit. What's true is that some muscle groups can be worked sufficiently only by machines. Lats are one, and for pitchers lats are extremely important. You'd think a pitcher would want to be overbuilt on the chest side, so that he could pull his arm forward as fast as possible while throwing the ball, but in fact it's more important to be well conditioned behind the arm. During follow-through, the lats flex in order to arrest the arm's forward motion. The majority of shoulder injuries come from overextension. All of this is a long way of explaining why I spend hours every week pulling a bar down over my head, and even more in the rower.

On the plus side, machines are great for phone calls. I always wear a headset while I row. This morning I spend half an hour on the phone with Izzy, who tells me she's going to stick with dance.

"I think it's the right decision," she says. "I mean, it's not something I'm going to do professionally, but it would be a waste to quit now. I'm finally good enough to enjoy myself instead of just remembering the steps."

"Who says you can't dance professionally, Iz?"

"Nobody. I just assume my life won't go in that direction."

"Why not? You can do anything you want."

"It's not like that, Dad. I'm not sure I'd want to be a dancer. You're always saying how risky it is to rely on your body."

"Did I say that?"

"Many times."

"It's good advice."

"Anyway, I wanted to tell you that I thought it over, and I forgive you for missing my recital. I understand how bad you must feel."

"Well, thanks. I would be there if I could."

"Just don't send a big flower arrangement like last time, okay?"

"What was wrong with the flowers?"

"They were beautiful, all those white lilies and roses, but the delivery guy propped it up on an easel. Mom said it was a funeral arrangement."

"Maybe they got the order mixed up."

"Maybe." I can tell she doesn't believe me. "Just be specific this year, okay?"

"Got it. No lilies, no easels."

"Thanks, Daddy. I love you."

We sign off, and I get back to my rowing.

A minute later, the phone rings again. It's Ratkiss.

"Johnny, I just got an inquiry from the Nippon Ham Fighters about your availability next year."

"You think I want to be a Ham Fighter?"

"Don't laugh, they're a first-class club. Perennial contenders in the Japanese Pacific League."

"I'm not an export, Todd, I'm a major-league pitcher."

"Right now you are, and with any luck you will be next year, too. That said, it doesn't hurt to have something to fall back on."

I'm not persuaded. I've seen how this goes. An aging major-league player starts talking to a Japanese team, and the rumor alone prompts the American clubs to write him off. They worry you're hiding an injury or something. It's bad news.

"My answer is no. Tell the Ham Fighters sayonara."

"How about we agree to table the discussion? I'm just afraid that if you say no you'll regret it come the off season." I hear him take a sip of something. "When you're trying to decide between a minor-league deal with the Astros and a nonroster invitation with Cleveland, you'll say, 'Hey, Todd, what about that Japanese team, the one that offered to match my last salary in San José, paid to a tax-preferred offshore account?' Because, you know, if you make the money abroad, you don't have to pay U.S. taxes."

"Fuck your tax-preferred account," I say, and I hang up. I know he has my best interest in mind, but sometimes you have to remind your agent that he works for you, not the other way around.

# 30

Tonight's game is a 7:05 start, the first of a three-game series at home with the Arizona Diamondbacks. We jump to an early lead, scoring twice in the first inning. First time through the lineup, six of nine Bay Dogs reach base, and by the bottom of the third, we've chased Arizona's starter. But their bullpen holds up surprisingly well, allowing only one more run on three hits, and by the top of the eighth the score is 3–2 in our favor. After Arizona's first two batters are retired, Skipper calls me in to face Alex Barrow, the D-backs' best hitter. Barrow has been in the league three years, and because we're in the same division, I've faced him numerous times. He has an excellent eye for a power hitter, and, unlike most young players, he's patient at the plate.

Skip hands me the ball with an admonishment to "keep it clean." He means: Don't hit him. Don't even brush him back, and certainly don't knock him down. Just get him out. That's the message. Given my performance in Colorado, it makes sense that Skip would be worried. But, all things considered, I'm probably in a better position to retire Barrow tonight than I have ever been. When you hit a batter on purpose, word gets around. The hitters I face are professionals, supposedly immune to psychological games, but sometimes a whisper about my supposed rage is enough to give me the edge.

I tuck my glove under my arm and start rubbing up the ball. I take my warm-up pitches, making sure not to smile or give any indication that I'm more stable than I was in Colorado. I even knock my head to the side a couple of times like I just got out of the pool—a nervous tic invented on the spot. It's pretty corny theater, but, like I said, the tiniest edge is all I need.

Barrow steps in and eyes me cautiously. He does that thing where he windmills his bat and pauses with his right arm extended, angling the bat toward the mound like a sword. When I step onto the rubber, he returns the bat to his shoulder. Game on.

I get two quick strikes on inside fastballs that he fouls back into the screen. Modigliani wants to proceed according to plan, with a changeup low and inside, but I shake him off. With the count 0-2, I want to play with him a little. Eventually, Diggy figures out what I have in mind, and I deliver: a slider outside, about a foot off the plate, that bounces and sends up a puff of dust. Diggy crabs to his left and the ball caroms off his chest protector. Because there are no runners on base, he just ignores the ball—dirty now, probably scuffed—and requests a new one from the plate umpire. He glares at me, and I glare back—but not because I'm angry at Diggy. I couldn't give a shit about Diggy. This is all part of the theater. If I can convince Barrow that I'm not following the plan, that I'm off my game tonight, or, even better, that I'm mentally unhinged, then I maintain the advantage. I walk off the mound a couple of paces on the third-base side, rubbing up the new ball. I return to the mound and do a little landscaping with my toe on the landing spot.

The count is now 1-2. Again Diggy calls for the inside change, and again I shake him off. Now he's honest-to-God pissed, but I don't care. I'm in charge. I throw another slider in the dirt that Barrow takes for ball two. This time Diggy doesn't bother to scramble; the ball goes all the way to the backstop.

Again with a new ball, I walk off the mound on the first-base side. I pretend to see something in the grass—stray napkin? used condom?—and bend down, touch the grass, straighten up, and climb the mound. By this point, Barrow is totally confused. He windmills his bat once, then twice, pausing at maximum extension, swinging through. He kicks the dirt with his back foot, spits. He looks down the line to the third-base coach, who dutifully repeats the sign, even though everyone in the ballpark knows Barrow is clear to swing away.

I plant my left foot on the rubber and stare in. For the third time, Diggy gives the signal for the changeup low and inside. I shake him off, and then let him cycle through all the signs, refusing them all one by one. When he returns to the change, I nod. He taps his right thigh, indicating inside. I nod. He straightens his mask and sets up behind Barrow's left knee. I stretch, set, and deliver. It's a perfect pitch, a straight change that comes in ten miles per hour slower than anything I've thrown so far, and barely a foot off the ground. Barrow is a mile in front but still manages to make contact, tapping a weak grounder to short. Ordoñez charges. He scoops it up. His throw beats Barrow by a step and a half.

To hell with Todd Ratkiss. I can't give this up. Ultimately, I will have to retire—the human body can't do this forever—but not yet. I learned to throw when I was five or six years old, but I didn't learn to pitch until my thirties. All that knowledge, all that technique will vanish if I quit. Maybe I flatter myself by this comparison, but it's like asking a surgeon to quit doing operations just when he figures out how to cut without leaving scars.

We hang on to win by one. Earlier in the day, the Dodgers lost in St. Louis, so we're back within a game of first place.

After the game, I shower quickly and take the elevator upstairs, hoping to speak with Jock Marlborough. I find him in the press box, grazing the remnants of the deli tray.

"Got a minute?" I ask.

"Something tells me this ain't good news." His voice is uncharacteristically raw and raspy, like he hasn't been sleeping. With the bulging skin under his eyes, he looks like an elderly Labrador retriever. "Let's go in the booth," he says.

I follow him through a series of doors, down a short hallway to the broadcast booth, or what Jock calls, on the air, the "best seat in the house." It's right behind home plate, on the luxury level between the stadium's two main seating decks. I tend to think that the dugout is a better seat than the broadcast booth, but this isn't bad. A technician in headphones is typing on a laptop. Jock asks him to leave, and then it's just us, looking out over the thousands of empty seats. Cleaning crews move up and down the rows like ants. On the field, the grounds crew is placing the protective tarp on the mound.

"Lay it on me." Jock leans back in his swivel chair, placing his palms on his belly. I notice that his hands are tiny, with stubby little fingers. Hands made for radio, I guess you could say.

"I have a contact at the Marriott in Daly City, and he showed me some tape from the realtors' meeting last week."

"And?"

"You were right. She's fooling around."

"Is it Jim Hunt?"

"White man, your age . . . looks sort of like Ed McMahon?"

"I'll be damned. Of all the realtors to screw, she chooses Hunt. With all the swinging dicks in that office, all the top producers . . . I don't know how much you know about real estate, Adcock, but those bastards are competitive. Lots of testosterone—and cologne. She could have had some young stud, some hot slugger, but instead she chooses this guy."

"Do you know him personally?"

"Oh, sure, we go back. We used to have dinner with the Hunts two, three times a week in the off season. We're neighbors. I never liked Jim, but Eileen, his wife, was a real looker, just a tremendous, tremendous piece of ass. She had this way of giving head. . . ."

"So you're sleeping with his wife, too?"

Marlborough shakes his head. "Eileen passed away six years ago. Breast cancer." This isn't the first time a client has turned me loose with only half the story, but I can't say I've ever had a twist like this. I'm not sure what to say.

"Tell me," Marlborough says after a few moments' consideration. "Did she dress up?"

"She looked nice," I say diplomatically. "Double-breasted suit. Pearls."

He looks me in the eye. "I mean costumes."

"She had a room at the hotel. After her presentation, she went back and changed into a maid's uniform." I pause. "It's not the first time, I'm guessing."

"No, it's not."

I want to tell him it seldom is, but what good will that do? It's not my job to console. Marlborough wanted an answer, and he got one.

The enormous (cuckolded, adulterous) play-by-play man leans forward in his chair and puts his hands on his knees. "What do I owe you, Adcock?"

"Nothing," I say. "The first one's free."

"And the next?"

"Next time, just talk to your wife."

"There must be something I can do for you."

"There is one thing," I say. "I'm planning a party, something small with a few friends—how hard would it be to borrow a skybox for a night?"

# 31

After a bit more negotiation with Jock Marlborough, I leave the stadium and summon an Uber. Tonight's driver is a gangly Vietnamese kid in a plug-in hybrid.

"Airport," I say. "General Aviation."

"No bags?"

"Not tonight."

Fifteen minutes later, I'm in the GA parking lot at San José's Norman Mineta Airport. Mineta was a congressman from San José before he joined the Bush administration and became, on 9/11, the guy who famously ordered all aircraft to land. "Bring them all down," Mineta said, and the planes came down. (And he was glad of the deed.) The GA parking lot is full of Teslas and 7 Series Beemers with turbocharged engines. Also plenty of Ubers with groomed, butlerish men standing in the crooks of open doors.

"Right here is good," I say to the kid driver. We won't be taking any trips to the gun shop tonight, although I might feel more secure if we did. I shut the door, and the little car rolls silently into the night.

Erica is waiting for me, and together we walk across the tarmac to Tiff's plane.

"Busy week?" I ask.

Erica rolls her eyes. "You have no idea."

She shows me into the main stateroom, where Tiff is scampering around, looking for something between the cushions of the armchairs. Tonight she's dressed like a homegirl, with dark lipstick, gobs of eye makeup, and hair pulled into a tight ponytail on top of her head. Her pink velour tracksuit has the initials *T.T.* spelled out in rhinestones across the chest.

"Evening, Tiff."

"Johnny, come in." She holds open the door to her stateroom, and I follow her inside. The bed is unmade and covered with all kinds of clothes, women's and men's. Several dozen pairs of shoes are lined up along the wall. At the foot of the bed are a barber's chair and a mirrored vanity. I find the disarray unnerving. Tiff Tate doesn't strike me as a neat freak, but I am surprised she would let anyone glimpse this side of her life.

"Forgive the mess," she says. Tiff clears clothes off the barber's chair. "Here, sit."

"What about you?" I look around. There are no other chairs in the room.

"It's fine. I'll kneel." She does, and looks comfortable. I am not. The combination of the teenage-bedroom disorder and Tiff's J-Lo getup makes me feel like the clueless boyfriend in an after-school special about teen pregnancy.

"So," she says, finally catching her breath. "I have to say, I was thrilled when you called. I thought you'd never speak to me again."

"Connie left me."

Tiff shrugs. "Don't take it personally. Ballplayers and librarians don't mix."

"Do you know that for a fact? Have you had clients who dated librarians?"

"You're the first."

"I'm not your client. It's the other way around, remember?"

Tiff looks at me. "What did you tell her?"

"I told her that you tricked me."

"What about the doll?"

"I didn't have the heart to mention it. I explained that she is not, and never was, in any danger."

"Is she back in Denver?"

"She's not going back. If you can get someone over there to clean the apartment, I can arrange to have it opened."

"I'll do that." Her eyes well up. "I don't deserve this, but thank you."

"One more thing—I have an idea about La Loba, a way for you to make peace. It's simple, really: you two need to sit down and talk."

Tiff gives the corner of her eye a surgical wipe with the back of her hand. "This isn't the UN, Adcock. La Loba is a criminal, and I'm—well, you know what I am."

*Actually,* I think, *I have no idea what you are.*

"Let me arrange a meeting."

"You're welcome to try, but I can assure you she doesn't want to talk."

"Just trust me. I can get her to come."

# 32

Back at home, I turn on ESPN and watch highlights from today's games. I call this baseball pornography, because what you see on *SportsCenter* is as much like a real ballgame as porn is like sex. Most of a game is foreplay, but ESPN just airs the money shots: the home runs, third strikes, and double plays. It can be stimulating to a point, but after that it's just noise. The noise stage is what I like best. More than silence or reading or meditation, it helps me think.

I review the details of the case—what I know, and what is left to discover. I start at the beginning, when Tiff approached me in the bullpen dressed as a field reporter. She said she had a client, Yonel Ruiz, whose family was being held hostage in Cuba by the criminals who smuggled him off the island. That turned out to be a lie. Tiff smuggled Ruiz out of Cuba, which wouldn't have been a big deal except that she aggravated the woman who controls the Cuban smuggling racket, a ruthless operator named La Loba. Tiff tried to apologize to La Loba, but La Loba wanted her dead as a warning to future competitors. Frightened for her life, Tiff hired me—ostensibly, to find Ruiz's tormentors; actually, she wanted me to kill La Loba, but first she had to give me a motive. So she placed an anonymous call to my cell phone, which allowed me to witness La Loba chopping up her latest victim. Then she sent Connie away under a false premise of danger. She put a blood-filled sex doll in Connie's living room, and had her driver take me there after helping me buy a pistol. I was supposed to put two and two together and run out and kill La Loba. But I found Connie's airline itinerary and concluded, correctly, that Connie wasn't dead, just AWOL. When Tiff found out that I'd given my gun to her driver and flown back to California, she became desperate, dressed up like Connie, and threw herself on my doorstep to confess and beg for help.

Meanwhile, bodies are piling up—and not just the competitors chopped up by La Loba. My friend Erik Magnusson was killed in his office at Coors Field, hanged from the ceiling joists like a game animal. A few days later, two employees of a Sonoma winery were murdered the same way. In the latter incident, the killer lured me to the scene of the crime and then called the police—clearly an attempt to set me up.

What else? The night after Magnusson was killed, I saw Ruiz and La Loba together in a French restaurant in Denver. She claimed to be his sister. They left before placing an order. Is it possible that La Loba was negotiating with Ruiz for access to Tiff? When I, ahem, visited her later that night, she was as interested in Tiff as she was in me. Maybe more.

There are other bits and pieces: the chipped tooth I found in the video room where Magnusson was killed; Mags's musings on the whiteboard about Ruiz and someone named Pascual Alcalá; the strange posthumous note from Mags in which he admits to lying about the phone threat. You might also say the bottle of wine from Domaine Amphora was a clue, but at this point I think it was just a lure.

The big question for me is Mags. I feel bad for Tiff—she was in over her head the minute she set sights on Cuba—but, let's be honest, Mags is the one who got screwed here. He didn't ask to be caught up in identity fraud when he offered his spare bedroom to Yonel Ruiz. I find it hard to believe he was killed simply because he knew that Ruiz had changed his name, but unless Mags produces another letter from beyond the grave, that's my hypothesis.

Of course, all of the above may change tomorrow night. Jock Marlborough texted with the news that he has secured a suite for my "party" after the game. I call him to confirm. "It's the Comcast suite, right?"

"No, the one next door. It belongs to one of the owners. When do you need it?"

"Is eleven-thirty okay?"

"I don't think that will be a problem," he says. "Listen, Johnny, I wanted to thank you again. I confronted Kitty about Jim Hunt, and she confessed the whole thing."

"Did she?"

"And get this: she says Jim is a selfish lover and she wants me back."

"That's great news." I pause. "Is it great news?"

"We'll see. I'm not much of a Casanova myself. You know, women become more difficult to please as they get older. Could be Jim Hunt is twice the lover I am at this point and nobody's good enough for Kitty."

I picture Jim Hunt pounding away behind Kitty Marlborough, his doughy tits swinging in time with hers. When I was at Fullerton, there was a band called The Lowest Pair that played house parties off campus. Those guys would have loved Kitty and Hunt. Nothing's more punk than old people fucking.

"Well, I'm glad," I say. "I hope it works out for you and Kitty." Matrimonial cases don't usually end in happy reunions. Usually, they catalyze divorce. It's refreshing to be on the other side for a change.

# 33

Next morning, when I arrive at the Bay Dogs' clubhouse, the pregame rituals are already under way. Modigliani is on the trainer's table, where an assistant in a yellow polo shirt massages his haunches. The young assistant's face remains expressionless even when he stretches Diggy's leg high in the air, leaning on the limb with most of his weight, so his nose comes within inches of the catcher's naked ass. The term "jock sniffer" isn't a figure of speech. The assistant trainer probably could have been a doctor, and look what he's doing instead.

I walk down the center aisle, nodding to teammates relaxing in front of their lockers. At a folding table in the middle of the room, Chichi Ordoñez is playing poker with two rookies. No one but a rookie would play cards with Ordoñez, a wiry Puerto Rican with the quickest hands on the team. All the veterans know he cheats. The young guys might know it, too, but what are they going to do? Sometimes you have to pay your dues in real money.

"Hey, Adcock," Ordoñez says. "You better hurry if you want to say something to your boy Cunningham. He's on his way to Fresno."

It was bound to happen. It's been five days since Thick Will went to see Tiff Tate, and, batting-practice heroics notwithstanding, the makeover hasn't made a difference in his hitting. Skipper has been sitting him against lefties, platooning him with Joaquín Morales, our right-handed utility infielder. But Will hasn't hit righties, either. He's mired in a one-for-twenty stretch, with an alarming number of strikeouts. I feel like, as soon as he steps into the batter's box, he's down 0-2. He continues to stroke the ball in BP, suggesting that the problem isn't physical. If Magnusson were still around, I would have asked his advice.

I find Cunningham packing the contents of his locker into a black tote bag. He's wearing one of Tiff's tracksuits. His movements are deliberate, head hanging low over his work. His neighbors—the players with lockers on either side of his— are conveniently occupied elsewhere. They'll come back once he's gone. Baseball players think failure is an infectious disease. Harsh as that may sound to laypeople, there's some truth to it, psychologically.

"I heard the news, Will."

He twists his head to stare at me with one eye. "I don't blame them," he says. "I would have sent me down, too."

"You had an option left?"

"Yeah. Last one, though."

Every professional baseball contract includes a certain number of "options," or times that the club can send the player back down to the minor leagues.

"It's okay," I say. "You're going to crush it down there. We'll see you back in a month." I certainly hope it works out that way, but the truth is that Will's facing a tough road back to the majors. Because he is now out of options, it will be even more difficult for him to get promoted. The club knows that if they call him up again they must either keep him on the big-league roster permanently or risk losing him to another club on the waiver wire.

"Don't get discouraged if it doesn't happen right away," I say. "It could take a few weeks to find your groove."

"What groove?" Will says. "I have no groove."

"Take a walk with me."

"Nah, I gotta pack up—"

"Five minutes. Come."

I lead him up the tunnel to the dugout. At this hour, the groundskeepers have the field to themselves. A long hose connected to a pulsating sprinkler chops water over the outfield grass. Will and I stand behind home plate, near the Bay Dogs' on-deck circle.

"Look at that." I point to an LCD screen in right-center field. It's displaying an ad for a hotel chain in which a comely young brunette settles her head onto a feather pillow. Below this, the hotel's slogan appears in white letters. "Will, read me what it says on that screen."

Will squints. "*Mission Hotels, let us fuck you in tonight.* Hold on—is that for real?"

The "f" is supposed to be a "t," but a few of the pixels are broken thanks to one of Will's batting-practice rockets. "You did that," I say. "With your bat."

"No shit."

"Now everyone knows what you're capable of. There's the proof right there."

I'm not sure if he believes me—if self-confidence was so easy to fix, we'd have no need for psychotherapy—but I think I see a little spring in his step as he heads back down the tunnel.

# 34

We win the game, 6–4, and move into a tie for first place. I don't pitch, which is a good thing, because by the seventh-inning stretch my mind is already upstairs. At 11:00 p.m., as the cleaning crew crawls the seats, I make my way to the club level. A skybox is really two spaces. There's the balcony, where twelve stadium seats are arranged in two rows, and out there, with a cup of beer in your hand and some peanut shells under your feet, it might be possible to forget for a few moments how truly, unbelievably rich you are. Inside is another story. Inside, there's no forgetting. Imagine you're a middle-school boy and someone tells you that you're going to be a billionaire when you grow up. You will be able to buy whatever you want and put it in a private room at your favorite major-league baseball stadium. What would be on that list? Arcade games? Multiple cinema-sized TV screens? Framed posters of *SI* swimsuit models? Add in a few items that a twelve-year-old might not have considered, like a full bar, a mirror-topped coffee table, and a cream leather sectional couch, and you've just decorated your very own luxury suite.

It's a surprisingly versatile space, with enough room for a corporate team-building exercise, a saucy game of Twister—whatever strikes your fancy. The rent runs thousands per game, and you can't rent for just one game. Most of the suites are leased by corporations, but this one, as Jock pointed out, is the private redoubt of Rob LaPlante, a reality-TV mogul who joined the Bay Dogs' ownership group several years ago. LaPlante is known as the most sociable and down-to-earth of the owners, a genuinely friendly guy who never takes for granted that he is living out his childhood fantasy. On the other hand, he's kind of a sleaze. He made his fortune with the *Completely Naked!!!* series of reality shows, in which contestants perform everyday tasks such as folding laundry, making dinner, and giving performance reviews to employees . . . in the nude. When the shows first aired, the cable networks asked LaPlante to blur out nipples and genitals, but eventually he stopped doing it and discovered that nobody complained. Now he owns the Bay Dogs. We all keep waiting for the cameras to arrive with orders to strip, but so far he has kept us in uniforms.

My setup is minimal. I draw the drapes over the glass wall for privacy and sink some bottled waters and sodas into a tub of ice set out earlier by the catering staff. Marlborough made sure I understood that there would be no waiters available at this time of night. I told him that this was fine, that it was just a meeting.

Just a meeting with two of my closest friends.

I check my phone. There's a text from Enriqueta. She's downstairs. I leave the suite and walk to a bank of private elevators. During business hours, there's an usher sitting in the elevator, an older African American man in a straw hat and a blue-and-yellow Bay Dogs vest. You wouldn't think a stadium built in the early 2000s would need an elevator operator (come to think of it, you don't need an operator for any elevator built since World War II), but you also don't need an old man to hand you a towel in the bathroom at your country club. It's bizarre what rich people require.

The elevator opens onto a secret food court under the stands, available only to field-box and luxury-suite ticket holders. Here the ultra-rich can purchase the same fare as elsewhere in the stadium, but without the long lines and prying eyes of the hoi polloi. At this hour, the counters for hot dogs and garlic fries are dark and silent. The concierge desk, normally bursting with bright helpful blondes, lies empty. I walk to the VIP entrance, a surprisingly inconspicuous portal that is staffed by a security guard 24/7. Per MLB rules, there is a metal detector over the door. Tonight, I'm grateful for the extra caution.

I press the crash bar to open the door, and there stands La Loba, chatting amiably in Spanish with the guard. She is dressed like a sexual cat burglar, in black from her skintight turtleneck to her cigarette jeans. Her riot of hair has been tamed somewhat, braided loosely and twisted up. She's wearing dark lipstick, mauve shadow, and a thick stripe of coal-black liner around each of her mismatched eyes. She does not smile when she sees me, but simply parts ways with the guard, walks to my side, and says in Spanish, *"Are we ready?"*

*"Everything is ready,"* I say.

*"You told her I'm coming?"*

*"It's just as we discussed. She thinks I'm bringing a hired girl."*

Now Enriqueta smiles—a devilish grin that makes her eyes sparkle, the blue one a little more than the brown. *"Very good,"* she says. *"I'm excited to see you again, Adcock."*

I don't know if she saw me running away from the warehouse that night after my gun went off. If she did, she hasn't let on, just as I haven't let on that I know her as anything other than Yonel Ruiz's sister.

The elevator whisks us upstairs. The hallway of billionaires is deserted; the carpeted floor masks our footsteps. We stop in front of a door marked JOHN ROCKENBUSH.

*"Who's Rockenbush?"* Enriqueta asks.

*"Nobody,"* I say.

Rockenbush, of course, is Tiff's signal to me. I knock softly and push open the door. The room is nearly dark; the lights are much lower than I left them. Music drifts from speakers hidden in the walls. I clear my throat. "Hello, Tiff?"

A voice comes out of the dark: "Johnny! Did you bring a friend?"

A pinprick of blue light moves up and down in the darkness. At first I think it's a laser sight, but when I turn the lights up, I see that it's the LED tip of an e-cigarette. Tiff raises the device to her lips and inhales, making the end glow more brightly. She's barefoot, wearing a pair of white Capri shorts and a halter top. Her hair is blond again, this time held up in a French twist. She exhales a thin stream of vapor.

"I hope you don't mind the extra company," I say.

"Not at all. Come over here and introduce us."

Our plan was simple: I would lure La Loba here with the promise of Tiff, the prey she has been unable to catch. Then, assuming La Loba didn't immediately haul off and kill us both, Tiff would get her chance to beg for forgiveness. As a bonus, I would have the opportunity to ask La Loba about her relationship with Ruiz. I wasn't sure how the subterfuge of Enriqueta-as-prostitute would play out. I assumed that the charade would be over as soon as the two of them were face-to-face, but it appears that neither Tiff nor La Loba are willing to drop their roles just yet.

"I'm Enriqueta," La Loba says. Her English is heavily accented but confident. "What's your name?"

"I'm Tiff."

"Nice to meet you, Teef."

"You have a beautiful voice," Tiff says. "Are you from Mexico?"

"Venezuela."

"I hear Venezuela is an exciting country. Dangerous, though."

"It can be, if you don't know the right people." La Loba looks at me and then begins to pull up her turtleneck.

"Hold on," I say. "You don't have to do that."

Tiff stops me. "No, let me take a look at her. Go ahead, Enriqueta."

Putting the e-cigarette behind her ear, Tiff uses both hands to help La Loba pull the shirt over her head. She's wearing a black demi-cup bra, which Tiff helps her unclip.

Tiff says, "That's better, isn't it? We have all night to talk. Let's take some time to get to know one another."

"What do you have in mind?" Enriqueta asks.

"Nothing too serious. We'll just play around and see what happens."

La Loba looks at me. "What about him?"

"Join us, Johnny. Don't be a spoilsport." Keeping one eye trained on La Loba, Tiff walks over and unfastens my belt. Then she tugs the hem of my shirt and makes a little thumb gesture as if to say *Take it off.*

I obey. A minute later, the three of us are naked (or I suppose *Completely Naked!!!*) in the empty skybox. I've never felt more awkward. A Twister mat would be a welcome addition at this point.

"Give me a hand with the sofa," Tiff says. "These things turn into beds, if I remember correctly." She begins tossing cushions over the back of the couch. Sure enough, there's a handle.

Foldout beds: another must-have for the billionaire's tree house.

"We're going to play before we talk?" I ask Tiff, who is now kneeling on the bed with an unmistakable look in her eye.

"Why not?" she says. "I'm in no hurry."

I don't understand why she's pushing this angle. She knew La Loba was going to be playing the part of a prostitute, but that was only a ploy to get her up here. Maybe Tiff was concerned that La Loba would be carrying a gun and wanted to orchestrate a strip search? I should have told her about the metal detector at the VIP entrance.

La Loba follows Tiff onto the bed. "I prefer dark," she says.

"Johnny," Tiff says, "would you mind turning down the lights?"

Against my better judgment, I lower the fader, and instantly I regret it. Before my eyes can adjust to the darkness, someone sweeps out my legs, and I fall to the carpet on my hands and knees. Then I feel the pinch of a zip-tie around my ankles. I eventually struggle to my feet, but I'm hobbled and I can't see a thing. I smell perfume—Tiff's and La Loba's—and I hear a struggle somewhere to my left.

In Spanish, I say, *"Enriqueta, where are you?"*

*"Here, papi,"* comes a voice below me and to the left. I lower myself in that direction, but find nothing.

*"I have something to ask you,"* I say.

Suddenly there's a palm on my chest, and I'm knocked backward. With my ankles tied, I topple like a bowling pin. I hear a voice to my right: *"Where did you go, Johnny?"*

I roll to the spot where I heard the voice. Again—nothing.

*"Who is Pascual Alcalá?"* I ask the darkness.

Hands emerge to grab my balls. The voice whispers, maybe six inches from my ear, *"Who told you about Alcalá?"*

*"You'd like to know, wouldn't you?"* I whisper.

Enriqueta squeezes my junk. *"It's not what you think,"* she says.

*"What, Alcalá?"*

*"Yes."*

She releases me, and I hear footsteps on the carpet.

"Tiff!" I shout. "Turn on the lights!"

I stumble around blindly, chasing the sound of the footsteps. Then a voice in my ear—a very different voice—says, "She's got Tiff." It takes me a second to remember the earpiece. "In

186

her hand," Briggman says calmly. "It looks like a noose of some kind."

I hear the struggle in front of me, and this time Enriqueta is too preoccupied to play hide-and-seek. I grab both women— one arm around each—and pull them apart, pinning them to my sides.

Through the earpiece, Briggman guides me: "Suspect is in your left arm."

I let go of Tiff and pin La Loba to the bed. Tiff switches on the lights. In La Loba's left hand is a miniature garrote made of fishing line and a three-inch length of what looks like a broken chopstick. I take the weapon and twist her arm behind her back. She resists, but when she realizes she can't overpower me, she screams.

Try to imagine what this scene must look like to Briggman, alone in his control room in Salt Lake City: three naked humans in the dark, a virtual flashlight lighting up the one with the biggest hair. OmniSentry's sales rep said he didn't know if the system would work with remote feeds, and he didn't know about darkness, either. I think we have answers to both questions.

Tiff takes a knife from the bar and frees my legs. Then she stands in front of La Loba, both of them naked, Tiff's eyes big and glossy like she's going to cry. "Did you get my messages?" she says. "Didn't Yonel tell you? I'm done. You win."

La Loba shakes her head. "It doesn't work that way, Teef."

"But you have to believe me!"

"You say you're sorry, and I believe you. You say you won't do it again, and I believe that, too. But you made me look weak. Too many people know what you got away with. They are like cockroaches now, all over the island, looking for players to sign. I will not fight pests. The world must know what happens when you fail to respect La Loba."

She wriggles free, but I don't bother to seize her again. I've already taken her weapon. What harm is she now? She shakes out her arm.

"I didn't mean to disrespect you," Tiff pleads. "Had I known you were operating in Cuba, I never would have approached Yonel."

La Loba snorts. "I should let you live, just to see what happens when the truth comes out."

"What truth?" Tiff asks.

"Ask the detective!"

Tiff looks at me, but before I can answer, the door of the suite flies open. I recognize La Loba's assistant from the warehouse, the guy with the harelip scar. He stands in the doorway with a pistol. I dive behind another section of the sofa, but Tiff is slower to react. There's a loud crack, and she collapses onto the Berber carpet.

# 35

La Loba covers herself with a sheet, grabs her clothes, and leaves with the driver while I'm scouring the floor for my pants. When I find them, I dig out my phone and call 911. Tiff is unconscious and bleeding heavily. The bullet hole is on the right side of her chest, just below the clavicle.

"Nine-one-one, what's your emergency?"

"My friend has been shot."

"Is the victim conscious?"

"No, but she's breathing."

I hear typing. "I'm showing that you are at the ballpark downtown. Is that correct?"

"Yeah, we're on the club level. Suite Eighteen."

More typing. "A paramedic unit is on its way."

Almost as soon as she says it, I hear a siren, and then another. I dress hastily. Tiff's breathing slows. I kneel over her. Thanks to baseball, I never had to learn CPR. I've had highly trained professionals within earshot at all times since I was in my teens. I apply pressure to the wound, but that does nothing but cover my hands in blood. Real blood this time, Tiff. Real blood.

Then I hear voices in the hall. The door opens hard and

slams into the wall. It's not just the cavalry but the whole damn army: two EMTs with a stretcher, two firefighters, and four uniformed police, plus a couple of frightened stadium-security guards.

The EMTs rush to Tiff's side, perform a quick assessment, and lift her onto the stretcher. One hangs a plasma bag, another inserts an IV. Away she goes. Nobody makes much of the fact that the victim is stark naked—or that there's a foldout bed with rumpled sheets in the middle of the room—but it can't look good for me. I find myself walled off by cops.

"Are you Rockenbush?" the police sergeant asks me. He has a thick mustache, and a throbbing vein on his right temple.

"I'm Adcock. I work here."

The sergeant frowns. "That's how it goes, huh? Anybody gets to use these rooms when there's no game?"

"There was a game tonight," says a deputy with a white note-pad. "Dogs won, 6–4." The deputy looks at me. "Hey, wait a minute. You're that reliever. Remind me your name?"

"I told you, it's Adcock."

"Adcock, right! The lefty."

The sergeant is unimpressed. "Mr. Adcock, we're going to need to ask you some questions. But before we do that, I need to know if you'd like to have an attorney present."

Someone pushes through the wall of cops—a familiar lan-tern jaw perched atop a navy-blue suit. "Sergeant Fahey, cor-rect?" Feldspar shows the cop a badge—a badge!—and shakes his hand with brisk professional vigor. "I'm Jim Feldspar, Director of Personnel Security for Major League Baseball. If you wouldn't mind, sir, may I have a word with Mr. Adcock real quick?"

Fahey must be on the payroll, or at least in the ticket pool, because he takes his men and retreats into the hall. I mean, there is blood drying on the carpet and a suspect in the room. That's how good Jim Feldspar is. It pains me to say it, but it's true.

As soon as the cops are out of earshot, he lays into me: "You've got to be kidding—what the hell are you doing? You're like what's her name . . . Typhoid Mary? Everywhere you frickin' go, somebody turns up dead."

"Did she die?" Barely a minute has elapsed since the EMTs whisked Tiff away. It's possible Feldspar overheard something in the hall.

"I don't know. What I do know is that you're finished. Do you understand? I'm going to recommend the strongest sanctions possible. You should be banned, full stop. No contact with baseball players, no coaching or scouting. Definitely no playing. Now, maybe the commissioner in his infinite mercy will disagree, but I don't think so. We can't have people getting shot in luxury boxes. You had fair warning, my friend."

"You did warn me," I say, "but I just walked into this mess. . . ."

"You walked into nothing. You don't even have your shoes on." He looks around the suite at the sofa cushions flung willy-nilly, the pullout bed. "I don't even want to know what was going on in here."

"You have every right to be suspicious. But the thing is, that was my fiancée they just wheeled away."

"Spare me the bullshit, Adcock."

"Please. I need to know if she's going to make it. I need to get to the hospital."

Feldspar shakes his head. "Not going to happen tonight, big shot."

"Have a heart, Feldspar. Imagine your wife got shot. Please, I'll sign whatever you need me to sign, but let me go. You know I didn't shoot her."

Feldspar thinks it over. Toeing the carpet with his wing-tip oxfords, he discovers a condom wrapper, which he pins in place, holds for a moment, then kicks under the sofa.

"I'll talk to the cops," he says. "But as far as all this goes"—he waves his hand to indicate the stadium—"you're toast."

## 36

Feldspar pulls strings, and the police let me go. After a quick
stop in the clubhouse for a change of clothes, I retrieve my bike
from the players' lot. I head south, toward the hospital, in case
any of the cops are watching. As soon as I'm safely out of sight,
I pull over and check my phone. When I contacted Briggman
to ask about putting cameras in the skybox, he insisted that
I take two wireless tracking fobs, just in case. Now I'm glad
I did—and glad the meeting with Tiff and Enriqueta got as
touchy-feely as it did. The fobs look like tiny nicotine patches,
perhaps a centimeter in diameter, and they contain sensors that
allow them to be tracked by GPS. When the meeting took its
carnal turn, Briggman (in contact through my earpiece) urged
me to go ahead and stick the fobs. I did my best, sticking Tiff's
to her bra and Enriqueta's inside her left shoe.

I pull up the OmniSentry app and see a map of San José.
Two red dots appear. The first is not moving—that's Tiff, or
her clothing; she's inside a large outline labeled SILICON VALLEY
MEDICAL CENTER. The second dot is moving south along the
101. I put the bike in gear. Five minutes later, I'm doing ninety,
racing through the hills south of town. On a straightaway, I
steal a glance at the phone. The red dot has stopped moving.
It's fixed at a spot labeled SOUTH COUNTY AIRPORT. I know the

place, a little airstrip right off the highway, full of hobby planes and crop dusters serving the garlic fields of Gilroy. It's maybe twenty miles from my current position, so I pick up the pace. I'm doing a hundred, 110, 115. . . . Then, just as I enter Morgan Hill, I hear a siren. Red-and-blue lights appear behind me. There are others vehicles on the road, but none speeding like I am. There's no question he wants me. The cruiser flashes his brights and pulls me over just before the exit for the In-N-Out.

Then everything grinds to a halt. The patrolman takes his sweet time getting out of the car. He puts on the dome light, pretends to call something up on his computer screen. Great time to check Facebook, right? Why not?

I look at the phone. The dot moves slowly across the airport property. La Loba might be looking for parking, but more likely she's in a plane, and I'll bet a braid of Gilroy's finest that she isn't planning to spray any fields once she's airborne.

Finally, the patrolman walks over. "Please step off the bike, sir." He's a young guy, tall and strong. He reminds me more than a little of Thick Will Cunningham. "Stand next to the bike with your hands out to the side, like this."

I do as he says. He frisks me and finds nothing. Then he asks for my license and registration. I hand them over, along with a friendly smile.

"You think this is funny? I got you doing a hundred ten miles per hour in a sixty-five zone. That's reckless driving, thirty days minimum and a thousand bucks."

"I'm sorry," I say. "I wasn't paying attention to my speed. I'm in a hurry to get somewhere."

"We're all in a hurry." He looks at my license. "Do you like to gamble, Mr. Adcock?"

"What kind of gambling?"

"I like to bet on sports. I'll bet on football, basketball, horses, dogs. Even golf. But my favorite is baseball. Every year, during spring training, me and my buddy go to Vegas and put money on different teams to win the World Series. Last year he picked the Red Sox, and he won some dough."

"Losing always hurts."

"It does. And the year before, when the Giants won it all, he picked them, too. He's like a freakin' oracle, this friend of mine. We've known each other since grade school, and we've been scrapping ever since. You got any friends like that, Mr. Adcock?"

"I've had a few."

"What pisses me off is that my buddy is no smarter than me. He works graveyards at the 7-Eleven in King City. Is that the job of an intelligent man? But he keeps winning, which makes me think: Shoot, I should be able to do what he does. So, this year, when we took our trip to Vegas, I brought some swagger, some confidence, and when I made my World Series bet, I felt like, damn it, this is the one. You ever feel like that, like you just know something good is going to happen?"

I think about Keith the driver's parting words, back in Denver. He was so sure good things were coming to me. Then again, that might have been something Tiff paid him to say.

"I tend not to believe in that type of thing."

"I'm going to make you a bet, Mr. Adcock. Hopefully, what I just explained helps you understand how important this bet is to me. See, every year I pick the same team, my home team, the team I've loved ever since I was a kid. I'm talking about the Bay Dogs. Every year I pick the Dogs to win the Series, and every year I lose. Sometimes my buddy wins, and sometimes he doesn't, but I always lose. So let's make a deal, you and me. Let's agree that this year I'm going to win my bet. This year, the Bay Dogs are going to the Series. You think you can cover that bet, Mr. Adcock?"

"I can try."

"Well, I hope you do more than try, because, if I lose, then you lose. I'm going to write up this little incident here, this little reckless-driving felony, but I'm not going to put it in the books. I'm going to keep your name and address and registration and all that, and I'm going to wait until October to decide what to do. How does that feel? Does that seem like a fair deal to you?"

It's a rhetorical question. He doesn't even wait for me to respond. He walks back to his cruiser, presumably to copy down my information, and returns a minute later with my license and registration—and a baseball. It's covered with signatures, and I recognize many of them: Modigliani, Ordoñez, he's even got Will Cunningham. "If you wouldn't mind," he says, handing me a ballpoint pen.

"More bets?"

"Nope. That's just for you."

After twenty minutes by the side of the highway, the cop finally turns me loose. I check my phone, expecting to see the dot sailing away over the hills. Instead, I find that it's still flashing at the airport. I put the bike in gear.

I obey the speed limit until the patrolman is out of sight, then I haul ass. Before long I'm turning off in San Martin, where I park my bike and run up to the little terminal building. It's smaller than most bus stations, and there is no staff on duty at night. There are no lights out on the airfield, no planes taxiing.

I return to the phone map and zoom in as far as it will let me. The dot appears to be off to the side of the terminal, in a bank of lockers accessible from the outside.

Suddenly a text comes in: *Número 54, 26-3-31.*

# 37

The nurse at the desk tells me Tiff is due to have her surgical dressings changed, but I talk her into letting me visit.

"You're not from the police department, are you?" She's chubby but cute, wearing scrubs decorated with Grateful Dead bears.

"No, why do you ask?"

She rolls her eyes. "They were here all morning. She was so exhausted, I had to kick them out."

"I won't be long, I promise."

She leads me to the end of a long, curving hallway. Tiff's door is half open, and the nurse knocks perfunctorily before pushing it open. Tiff is awake and sitting up in bed. She has another visitor, as it turns out, a burly Latino in a dark dress shirt with several pounds of gold around his neck.

Yonel Ruiz stares at me. He narrows his eyes, then breaks off the stare and looks down at his hands, flexing his fists like a boxer. This dynamic feels familiar. Fine, I think. I'm ready, batter up.

"Adcock!" Tiff exclaims.

Ruiz leans over and kisses her gently on the forehead. "Quiet," he says. "You need to relax." His English is actually quite good—which makes sense to me now.

Tiff points to the bandage on her right shoulder. "The bullet hit me at an angle," she says. "Had it been a straight shot, I would have lost a lung. Maybe more."

"How do you feel?" I look straight at Tiff, ignoring Ruiz.

"Like I just had my shoulder shot off, but otherwise pretty good. I texted Yonel as soon as I woke up."

"We are in San Francisco this week," he says. "Four-game series with the Giants. I'll miss BP, but, you know, anything for Tiff."

"That's my motto," I say. "Anything for Tiff."

Tiff tries to laugh, but evidently it brings too much pain. She smiles and clutches her side.

"The doctor said she'll be back at work in a month," Ruiz says.

A month. Who will trim the beards while she's gone? Maybe La Loba will decide to go straight and start poaching Tiff's clients. Turnaround is fair play, right?

"He's right," I say, still not looking at Ruiz. "You need to relax. Take it easy for a while. Maybe you could use some time off."

"Don't take this the wrong way, Adcock, but that's such a male thing to say. Imagine I asked you to walk away from your career. What would your reaction be?"

"I don't have to imagine," I say. "People beg me to quit every day."

"I told La Loba I would give up smuggling, but damned if I'm going to walk away from styling. I worked too hard to get where I am. Name another woman in baseball with the power I have."

"I admire your conviction."

It comes out sounding more ironic than I intended. Tiff shoots back, "Come on, Adcock, isn't there anything you believe in? Any principle you believe is bigger than you?"

"Nearly everything is bigger than me."

"I'm serious."

"I believe in plenty of things. Honesty, fair play, justice. Which reminds me—I went after La Loba."

"You followed her out of the stadium?" Tiff sits up a little higher.

"I had a tracer on her clothing. There was one on yours, too. She and her driver went south, to a little airport near Gilroy. They took off before I got there."

Ruiz shakes his head. "She is too quick, every time."

"She left something for me at the airport."

I pull the manila folder from my knapsack and pull out a piece of paper, which I lay on Tiff's bed tray. It's a birth certificate from twenty-five years ago, marking the live birth of a seven-pound boy, Pascual Gutierrez de Alcalá. It lists both parents' names and occupations, and gives the place of birth: the municipality of Ponce, Puerto Rico.

"Who's Alcalá?" Ruiz asks.

I remove a stack of photos from the envelope and spread them out on the tray. The first is of a boy in ratty swim trunks, holding a donkey by a rope. Dense tropical foliage can be seen in the background. The next photo shows the same boy a few years older, playing on the beach. Finally, we see the boy in a high school baseball uniform with an aluminum bat over his shoulder. His physique is eye-catching even then, forearms thicker than the barrel of the bat, seamed with veins.

The boy is obviously Ruiz.

And that's only strike one.

I turn over the photo of the high school player. On the back, written in a neat cursive hand, is the name Pascual Alcalá, a uniform number, and the year 2008.

"I recognize myself in that photo," Ruiz says, "but I don't understand why it was signed like that. Someone must have gone to my school in Havana, taken a copy of this photo, and written the name of this other man."

"What school would that be?" I ask.

Ruiz gives me his batter's-box stare. "Santa Cruz de Olazábal, near the Plaza de—"

I flip another sheet onto the tray. It's a letter from the headmaster of the school he just named, stating with certainty that no student named Yonel Ruiz—or Pascual Alcalá, for that matter—ever attended his institution.

I lay down another sheet, this one from the census bureau of Cuba, stating that Yonel Ruiz was first counted in the province of La Habana in 2010. No person named Yonel Ruiz can be found anywhere in Cuba before that. In the 2010 report, Ruiz's age was stated as twenty-one, making him twenty-six or twenty-seven today.

"Government records are horrible in Cuba," Ruiz says. "This means nothing."

"Maybe not, but the government of Puerto Rico reported that Pascual Alcalá, whose name had appeared in the two previous censuses, was not found in the 2010 survey."

"Same problem, different island."

"She knew you'd say that." I bring out the final document, a twenty-page medical report from a company in Colorado. "This report establishes with ninety-nine-point-nine-percent certainty that the person known as Yonel Ruiz, living in Denver and employed by the Colorado Rockies Baseball Club, is descended from Maria and Jorge Alcalá of Ponce, Puerto Rico."

"How would they know?" Ruiz barks.

"Hair samples. It's all in the report."

"I don't believe any of it." Ruiz turns to Tiff. "And neither should you. These are lies told by a killer!"

"You grew up in Puerto Rico," I say. "You played baseball, and you hoped to sign a pro contract with an American club on your sixteenth birthday. Maybe you even enrolled in one of the baseball academies. But when your birthday came, nobody called."

"That's crazy. Who told you that?"

"A guy named Luis Peña, head scout for the Bay Dogs in the DR and Puerto Rico. I called him this morning. He said he remembers you—that is, he remembers Alcalá. He said when all the scouts passed you over you were crestfallen."

Ruiz looks at Tiff.

"It means upset," Tiff says.

"Here's what I think happened after that. Your parents said you weren't meant to play ball, that you were meant to learn a trade, or become a farmer. But you wouldn't give up the dream. You knew you had talent, and you'd heard about Cuban players attracting the interest of the Americans after their sixteenth birthdays. Sometimes long after. Because the Castro government prohibits emigration, those players weren't waiting around to be discovered. They had to make a reputation in the Cuban League first, then sneak off the island and sign. You weren't afraid of hard work. You were willing to put in your years. You had no doubt you could make a name for yourself in Cuba.

"That name turned out to be Yonel Ruiz. You arrived sometime before 2010 and eventually made your way to the Industriales, the Yankees of the Cuban League. You played well. By the time Tiff found you, Cuban baseball players had become a precious commodity, and you were well positioned to realize your dream. You liked Tiff's proposal to travel in disguise, because you were already comfortable using an assumed identity.

"Tiff did right by you. Here you are playing in the major leagues. Until recently, you had never even heard the name La Loba. But she knew about you, and, more important, she knew that someone else, someone other than her, had smuggled you out of Cuba. She found Tiff and set about trying to make an example of her. At the same time, she began gathering information on you. Imagine her surprise when she discovered that you weren't Cuban at all. I think this upset La Loba even more than Tiff's dabbling in her business. As any trader knows, the best way to lower the price of a commodity is to increase the supply, and you figured out a way to do that for Cuban ballplayers. Think what would happen if word got around the Caribbean that anyone could become the next Cuban phenomenon—even Puerto Ricans! Cuba would be flooded with talent, which would be great for the owners of the Cuban teams, but horrible for La Loba.

"So she assembled this file. She could have just mailed it to ESPN and been done with it. They would have broken the story, and you would have been exposed. But that wasn't enough for her. She wanted you to break the news yourself. She was waiting for you to go public and admit the crime, as a warning to players all over the Caribbean not to attempt what you did. That's what you were negotiating that night I saw you at the restaurant." I pause. "Your family isn't being held at gunpoint, are they?"

"They moved to Miami the week after I signed."

"So the hostage crisis—that's a story you made up for Tiff?"

Ruiz lowers his head.

Strike two.

"Yonel," Tiff says, "why didn't you tell me?"

"Where I'm from, you get signed when you're sixteen or you don't sign at all. Nobody wants a twenty-year-old player from Puerto Rico. This was the only way."

"Puerto Rico is part of the U.S.," Tiff says. "Does that mean you have a U.S. passport?"

Ruiz nods solemnly. "Correct."

"So I didn't need to smuggle you anywhere. . . ." She stops, but I follow her thought: if she hadn't smuggled Ruiz out of Cuba, she wouldn't have antagonized La Loba. For months, she's been blaming herself for the peril she's in. Without question she's guilty, but Ruiz shares much of the blame.

A nurse arrives with a bedpan. She says she can't wait any longer. We have to leave for a few minutes, but we can come right back.

"It's fine," I say. "I need to get going."

"Me, too," says Ruiz.

"Call me!" Tiff calls after us. I don't know who she means—me or Ruiz—and I really couldn't care.

# 38

It plays out exactly as I hoped. The elevator is near the nurses' desk, and while we're waiting, Ruiz asks if there's a stairwell.

"Good idea," I say. "Let's walk."

Realizing that he can't escape me—that we both need to get downstairs—Ruiz decides to wait. The elevator arrives, and we step inside. We're alone.

"What I couldn't figure out for the longest time," I say, "is how Erik Magnusson fit into this. I mean, he told me that you stayed with him last winter—but so what, right? Even if he knew you changed your name—hell, even if he knew you were Puerto Rican—that's no reason to kill him."

Ruiz stares at the floor numbers above the door.

"But Mags had fallen on hard times. I'm not sure you knew the full extent of it, but his wife left with the kids shortly before you came to stay at his house. I'm sure you know how tenuous the job of hitting instructor can be. One slump too many and he's out on the street. An unemployed former jock with a tarnished reputation."

Still no reaction from Ruiz. The bell dings for the third floor, and the doors open, but no one gets on. Maybe someone got tired of waiting and took the stairs.

"I think Magnusson was blackmailing you. I think he figured out about Pascual Alcalá, and he threatened to expose you. Maybe he kept raising his demands? I heard a story recently about another extortionist who did that. At any rate, you reached a breaking point, and you killed him in the video room. You hanged him from the ceiling to make it look like suicide. Later, when you realized the gravity of what you'd done, you began searching for a way to duck suspicion. You learned that Tiff had hired me. Given my reputation, you figured that I was no stranger to sticky situations. If you could frame me for a similar murder, the cops might pin the Magnusson job on me, too. You sent me a bottle of wine under Connie's return address, and arranged to have the tasting-room workers killed."

"Arranged how?"

"Come on, Ruiz. You make eight million a year. More with endorsements, thanks to Tiff. I'm sure you could find someone to do your dirty work."

The bell dings for the ground floor. Ruiz turns his head and says, as cool as can be, "You can't prove shit."

He smiles. I notice that his front tooth is broken.

"Maybe not," I say as we step out of the elevator. "But take a look at this." I pull out my phone and show him the picture I took of Magnusson's whiteboard. He killed Mags to keep his secret safe; if he'd erased the board, I never would have figured it out.

Ruiz looks at the photo but does not react. The hospital's main entrance is around the corner from the elevator lobby, and right up until the moment he takes that corner, Ruiz remains cocky. "I don't know why you're so upset," he says. "You would have killed that juicer, too."

And then he sees it, behind the sliding glass doors: the throng of police, the reporters with lights and cameras—and a tall, handsome man in a dark wool suit.

205

# 39

Jim Feldspar sits across from me in the air-conditioned conference room. We are in the Bay Dogs' administrative offices, a
part of the stadium I rarely visit. He is calling this meeting a
"debrief," but to me it feels like another interrogation. He writes
notes in his leather-clad legal pad, pausing now and then to
take sips from a sweating can of Diet Coke. I haven't touched
the glass of water in front of me.

Ruiz is in custody, but no charges have been announced.
The police sergeant at the hospital told reporters that Ruiz was
"a person of interest" in "a developing situation," and no details
were available right now. I get the feeling the cops are waiting
for direction from Feldspar. This is his prisoner, so to speak.

Feldspar sets the can on the table and looks up from his
notes. "So tell me, how did you figure out that Magnusson was
blackmailing Ruiz?"

"Just a lucky guess," I say. "I couldn't think of any other reason why Ruiz would have killed him."

Feldspar writes something down. "And you confronted Ruiz
in Miss Tate's room at the hospital?"

"No, it was after we left, in the elevator."

"But you were bluffing."

"About the blackmail, yes. But I'm positive he killed Magnusson."

"You have evidence?"

I pull the tooth from my jacket pocket and shoot it across the table to Feldspar. "I found that on the floor of the video room at Coors. It belongs to Ruiz. Check his mouth. Right lateral incisor."

Feldspar rotates the tooth with the tip of his pen. "You think Magnusson hit him?"

"I'd like to believe Mags wouldn't go down without a fight."

"So your scenario is that there was a scuffle in the video room, in which Ruiz lost a tooth. But Ruiz eventually overpowered Magnusson and strung him up from a ceiling joist."

"Something like that. You saw the body, not me."

More writing. "And you're suggesting that Ruiz's motive was blackmail. Magnusson discovered that Ruiz was lying about his identity."

"Check the whiteboard in the video room. Magnusson knew the score. Ruiz isn't Cuban. He's from Puerto Rico. He moved to Cuba and changed his name after he wasn't picked up as a sixteen-year-old."

Feldspar winces. "You're almost correct there. Actually, he did receive an offer from the Pirates, but only if he changed positions and became a pitcher. Apparently, Ruiz—or Alcalá, as he was known then—refused to do it."

"Hold on—you know Ruiz isn't Cuban?"

"It isn't public knowledge, but the commissioner's office knows, yes." He pauses. "You look surprised. Cuba is hot, Adcock. It's a fantastic story, with the sharks and the daring escapes. You can see how it's better for baseball if we let him be Cuban."

"I guess that's the difference between us," I say.

"Don't be naïve. You're in show business. Just ask your friend Tiff Tate. She gets it."

Tiff is going to be getting plenty, I realize, if Feldspar lets Ruiz "be Cuban." He wouldn't have to do much—maybe call his friends in the passport office, get them to delete the record of Pascual Alcalá. . . . If only Ruiz had known that Feldspar could hook him up, he might have spared Magnusson. It leaves a bad taste in my mouth. We Americans look down our noses at countries like Cuba, where truth is relative, but it's the same shit here: Feldspar is just Anibal Martín without the fedora and cigar.

"So you're going to let him get away with it?"

"With murder? No! Even if I wanted to, I couldn't fix that. We'll make sure he has a lawyer, but it doesn't look good for Ruiz at this point." He produces a plastic baggie from a pocket behind the legal pad and scoops up the tooth as though it were a dog turd.

"Can I go now?" I ask.

"Yes, you can. Pitch well tonight."

Oh, that. How nice of him to remember.

Feldspar adds, "Adcock, I appreciate what you did this morning. Calling me was not only the right thing to do, it was also a mark of maturity. I want you to know I won't forget it."

If I'm hearing him correctly, we're good. No more threats to shut me down. It's a pleasant surprise. But I still hate him.

# 40

Less than one week later, it appears that Jim Feldspar has already forgotten. I get a call from Todd Ratkiss, who informs me that the commissioner has received a recommendation from his security team that I be banned for life.

"Good news is that the union has already negotiated it down to administrative leave."

"What's administrative leave?"

"It's like the disabled list. You get paid, but you can't play."

"No way."

Ratkiss sighs. "Hasn't this gone far enough?"

"Let me handle it," I say.

I hang up and get Pete Gretsch on the line. Gretsch is someone I've known for a long time. Over the years, he has served in many different capacities at MLB's New York offices. Recently, he was appointed to the post of deputy commissioner. He's a trim man in his late fifties, with steel-colored hair and sharp eyes. He and his wife, a big-shot oncologist, live in Scarsdale with their two precocious teenage daughters. The girls play violin, first and second chairs in the Greater Westchester Youth Orchestra. Both have straight A's in all subjects (but especially science and math) and intend to follow their mother into the medical field, if Juilliard doesn't snatch them up first. In short, the Gretsches are your typical high-achieving Westchester County family.

Or so it would appear. Last year, Pete came to me with a dilemma. Turns out his elder daughter, June, had been keeping a secret from her parents. From everyone, really. It started with an innocuous middle-school project about money management, where each student got to invest a couple hundred bucks in an imaginary stock portfolio. Pete and his wife loved the idea so much they extended it, giving each of the girls a bit of real money to invest. They thought it would help teach them the value of a dollar, one of the hardest lessons to learn in a place like Scarsdale. The younger sister lost interest and cashed out her positions at the end of the school year, but Junie kept at it. She asked for more money to invest, and Pete agreed. Her results were excellent—what else could they be?—and before long Pete was transferring a thousand bucks into her brokerage account every month. Little did he know she was secretly wiring the money to an Irish sports book, where she had started playing horses and dogs. She moved on to European soccer and rugby, and by the time Pete discovered what she was doing, she was betting on half the Major League Baseball schedule every night. There are no hard-and-fast rules about family members gambling on games, but if Gretsch himself were caught gambling on baseball, he'd lose his job on the spot. The commissioner's office has a zero-tolerance policy—just ask Pete Rose. Gretsch knew he could handle Junie, but he needed my help getting her accounts to disappear. So I made some calls. A friend of mine who runs a small oddsmaking operation in Connecticut (no baseball, just NFL and college hoops) put me in touch with an English friend of his, a guy named Hamish who sounded, when we spoke over the phone, exactly like that auto-insurance gecko. A few days later, the Irish book transferred ownership of Junie's account to Hamish, who quietly cashed it out and wired the money to Pete—disguised as a speaking fee for a sports-management conference in Brussels.

When I call, Gretsch is already in bed, even though it's only ten-thirty. "This better be important," he says.

I skip the pleasantries: "Feldspar is recommending a life ban for yours truly."

"Why? What happened?"

"I was working a case and witnessed a shooting."

"Really? That's not so bad."

"It happened in the owner's skybox."

Gretsch exhales. "We work for the owners. You know that."

I like Gretsch. I don't want to be rough with him. But the clock is ticking. As we speak, Jim Feldspar is lining up his evidence: my involvement with Magnusson, the SOS call from Sonoma, the orgy in the skybox—not to mention all the trouble I got into last season. I imagine him printing out my crimes in a super-sized font and lovingly gluing the pages to foam-core boards for easy comprehension by the commissioner.

I can't lose to this guy, I just can't. So what choice do I have? I give Gretsch a little chin music. "How's Junie?" I say. Just like that.

"She's doing well," Gretsch says with a little hesitation. "She starts at Princeton in August."

"You and your wife must be so proud."

There's a beat of silence. "I'll do what I can," Gretsch says.

Two days later, the commissioner reaches his decision. In a confidential memo sent to the players' union and my agent, he writes: *John Adcock is a valued member of the Major League Baseball family. Like any family, we in baseball forgive mistakes. Punishment is time served.*

# 41

It's a Friday night in August, and the San Diego Padres are in town. It feels good to be with the team, back in the realm of the familiar. The sleeves of my blue undershirt hit my arms just above the elbow, just where I like them, and the cuff of my pants falls just so on the tops of my spikes. Even when the rest of your life makes no sense, you can depend on a uniform. Cops and pilots and UPS drivers know what I mean.

Stretching on the outfield grass with the other pitchers, I remember something Jock Marlborough likes to say: "Baseball is older than you." The statement is obviously true, but what I think he means is that baseball exists outside of time, with its own rhythm and a governing logic that extends beyond the rules of the game. The idiosyncratic but predictable rhythm of baseball regulates our lives. How could I quit this game? I couldn't live without the routine. But I shouldn't kid myself: it's a one-way love affair. Would baseball go on without me? You bet it would. Cemeteries are filled with dead ballplayers.

Speaking of dead players, the trial of Pascual Alcalá, aka Yonel Ruiz, lasts just three days before he is convicted of killing Magnusson and masterminding the murder of the Sonoma winery workers. The tooth turns out to be inadmissible, but the police find plenty of other incriminating evidence: phone records, security-card swipes, and written demands from Magnusson. Ruiz will never play baseball again, but Alcalá might—for the penitentiary team.

Tiff Tate fares almost as poorly as her lone smuggling project, and I'm not just referring to her reconstructed right shoulder. The criminal investigation of Ruiz revealed that Tiff engineered Ruiz's exit from Cuba and immigration into the United States. Federal authorities decided to bring human-trafficking charges against Tiff—charges her lawyers tried to get dismissed, arguing that Tiff hadn't broken any laws transporting Ruiz, a U.S. citizen, over the border. The federal judge was not persuaded. Eerily aping La Loba, the judge saw an opportunity to make an example of Tiff, and he let the charges stand. Her case is awaiting trial.

The Padres are mediocre again this year, but they have a few bright spots. Because they were basically out of the division race by All-Star break, management used the last half of the season to audition prospects on the big stage. Most of the fresh meat melted under pressure, or thrived for a quick week or two before the league identified their weak spots. However, one young Padre has been on a tear since the moment he arrived in San Diego, and no one has been able to check his ascent. His OPS is holding steady at 1.000-plus, with his on-base percentage climbing every week. In the absence of a better approach, some teams just award him first base two or three times a game. You'd think the kid was Barry Bonds. His name is Hernández, and I'll give my bag of sunflower seeds to the first person who identifies his country of origin. Hint: swim ninety miles south of Key West and you can't miss it.

The timing of Hernández's arrival was uncanny. It's almost like word reached Cuba that Ruiz was in trouble and they needed to send another five-tool man-child, pronto. One unfortunate note on Hernández is that his presence in the States means La Loba is still in business. With her sole competitor facing federal prosecution, there is only one way Hernández could have left Cuba. Somewhere out there, La Loba is still loading Zodiac boats with priests and players—and chopping up anyone else who tries to do the same.

That Hernández and I will face each other tonight is a foregone conclusion: he's one of the top left-handed hitters in the league. The only question is whether the game is close. As luck would have it, the score is tied at two in the top of the eighth, and when the Friars get the first runner on, the phone rings in the bullpen. By the time they bring me in, the bases are loaded. I'm not especially nervous, proof that the human body can become accustomed to virtually anything. My left knee tickles a bit when I push off, but it's late August, nearly September, and if a ticklish knee is your only complaint at this point in the season, you're doing well.

Skipper puts the ball in my glove and taps my ass. "Make him earn it," he says.

I like to think I can do better than that. "Make him earn it" sounds like Hernández is going to get his due, no matter what I throw, so I ought to fail with dignity, not by walking home a run. Modigliani has nothing to add. He trots back to the plate to receive my warm-up tosses. I put a little extra on them, just because. Maybe because I've been humiliated by enough Cubans (and fake Cubans) this month. Or because I'm not dead yet. Shit, maybe I just want to hear the mitt pop.

Javier Hernández is a thoroughbred, a black stallion. There is no such thing as a typical Cuban complexion. Ricky Ricardo was as white as a ghost. Hernández's skin is very dark. He shares Ruiz's musculature, but he's taller and a bit more graceful at the plate. Whereas Ruiz held his elbows close to the body, worrying the bat up and down like a piston, Hernández wags his bat playfully as he waits for the pitch. He swings with a higher-than-usual step, but he plants his foot quickly. It's a versatile approach, not especially vulnerable to off-speed pitches. The scouting report says to bust him in on the hands to start the count, to keep him from taking possession of the inner half of the plate. That's good advice, but it's boilerplate: it's what scouts write when they don't have any other advice to give. Work him in and out, mix your speeds. That's not a strategy; that's pitching.

The San José crowd goes silent as Hernández steps into the box. Diggy puts down a sign. He wants a slider outside, not the high-and-tight fastball that everyone in the ballpark expects. This is known as stealing strike one. It works best in the middle of the game, maybe the second time through the order, once the starter has established a pattern. Say you start all nine hitters with a fastball the first time through. That puts you in a position to steal a strike with a curve or a changeup, maybe. Big maybe, because if the batter isn't looking for a fastball, if he's considering taking the first pitch for no other reason than to drive up the pitch count, to put that extra mile on your arm, then he can just wait on your off-speed ball and drive it anywhere he likes. That's a medium-sized risk with nobody on base in the fifth inning, but it's a big fat risk in the eighth with the bases loaded.

On the other hand, this kid has been in the majors how long, two months? How many times has he seen a late-innings reliever try to steal a first strike? I'm 90 percent sure he's expecting a fastball. Diggy is 99 percent sure. It would be nice to have him down 0-1 without having shown him the heater. If it works, he won't know what to expect from the second pitch. Another breaking ball, or the inside fastball he expected on pitch number one?

I nod to accept Diggy's call. The runners take their leads. I look over my shoulder to stare down the guy on third, to freeze him so we have a play at the plate on a grounder. I set at the belt, kick, and deliver. I use a high three-quarters arm slot so that the pitch looks like a fastball out of my hand. The ball crosses the plate as a strike, but curls off the outside corner at the last second. Hernández begins his swing and plants his front foot early, just as he would for a fastball. But then he does something odd, something I've seen very few hitters manage to do: he slows the movement of his upper body so it trails the rotation of his hips. He still follows through with the swing, but he manages to put a few milliseconds between hips and shoulders. Now he's no longer out in front of the ball but right on top of it, or maybe even a little ahead, as he squares his shoulders and extends his arms. The ball explodes off the bat with a resonant crack and soars down the right-field line. It doesn't stop rising until it bounces off the concrete lip of the second deck, 350 feet from home plate. In foul territory.

I exhale. That's strike one.

I take a walk around the mound, rubbing up the new ball, as the runners retreat to their bases. The crowd chitters, but a strike is a strike, and Javier Hernández is down 0-1. I wouldn't say that we "stole" strike one, but he didn't hand it to us, either. To be honest, it was the kind of foul ball you want to forget as soon as you see it.

I climb the mound and plant my left foot on the rubber. Diggy hangs two, calling for another slider, but I shake him off. He cycles through the other signs: fastball in, fastball out, slider in the dirt. Finally, he returns to the original call, slider outside, and I accept. I'm hoping Hernández doesn't know what to think. *If he is going back to the same pitch again,* he should be asking himself, *why did he keep shaking off the catcher? Must be a fastball this time. But why so many signs? Maybe he throws a curve? No, the sheet said this guy has only a fastball, slider, and cutter. Jesus Christ!*

Yes, Jesus Christ. This is the bigs, the show, and I've been pitching here since you were in kindergarten. I deliver a second slider, two inches farther outside than the first. This one was never a strike, not from the moment it left my hand, but the poor kid is so confused he swings anyway.

Strike two.

This time I don't leave the mound. As soon as I receive the toss, I plant my foot on the rubber and stare in. Diggy wants a fastball up. A challenge pitch. In a way, this one is even more risky than the first-pitch slider, because my fastball isn't all that fast. On a good day I'm breaking ninety, but not by much. With two strikes, though, the strike zone expands, because Hernández won't want to be caught looking at strike three. No need, therefore, to put the ball over the plate. Anything close and he'll swing. I just have to make sure he misses.

I nod and check the runners. When I look back, Diggy is setting up inside. This isn't what I had in mind, so I step off. Everybody breathes. When I step back on, Diggy repeats the sign: fastball up. I shake it off, and I shake off all the other signs in the cycle until he starts adding direction, tapping his thigh to indicate inside or out. He never hits on the combination of pitch and location I want, so I step off again. Diggy stands up and runs out to the mound.

"The fuck?" he says after he pulls off his mask. "Are you waiting for an engraved invitation?"

"Fastball outside," I say through my glove. "Way outside, and shoulder high."

"Like a pitchout?"

"Almost, yeah."

Modigliani raises an eyebrow. There's no love between us, but I'd like to think we enjoy mutual respect. We're both veterans, and although I've never made an All-Star team, I'm sure Diggy recognizes that it takes a certain amount of skill to stick around fourteen seasons. Skill and wisdom: put them together and you get wile.

"All right," he says. "Just make sure he can't reach it."

He replaces his mask and trots back to the plate. He sets up a little outside, not enough to signal anything unusual. I set, check the runners. The guy on third bird-dogs me, making little head-fakes toward the plate, wiggling his fingers like he's Jackie Robinson. I stare him down, standing absolutely still, until he retreats to a reasonable lead.

I kick and deliver.

Diggy rises from his crouch before the ball even leaves my hand, and it's a good thing, because the pitch is higher than I intended. As I expected he would, Hernández swings, stretching his arms as far as they will go, almost throwing the bat at the ball. Already I know I'll be watching this in the video room after the game, whether or not it works out in my favor, just to know how in God's name he is able to extend his arms so far. Does he have another joint in there somewhere? Can he dislocate his shoulder on command? It seems to defy anatomy.

Somehow Hernández makes contact, but just barely. The end of the bat grazes the ball, a foul tip, which would have bought him another pitch—a foul is a foul, whether it goes 350 feet or zero—but today is an unlucky day for Mr. Hernández. Today the fox evades the hound. The glancing blow of the bat barely alters the pitch. The catcher knew what was coming, and he's standing there with an open mitt. Tipped and caught for strike three.

Welcome to the big leagues, Javier.

# 42

August becomes September, and the Bay Dogs hit their stride. We sweep three with the Padres and take three of four from the Nationals to close out the home stand. Reporters start to use the phrase "postseason potential" in articles about us. In fourteen years as a Bay Dog, I have been to the playoffs exactly twice, losing both times in the first round. My bet with the Highway Patrol notwithstanding, it's exciting to imagine playing in the postseason again—everything is brighter in October, louder and crisper. It would be nice to feel that thrill one more time before I retire. That said, my role is a small one. What happens in the eighth inning counts toward the final score, but there is usually one more inning after I pitch. Some relievers think of themselves as keystones, but I'm not holding up any bridges. I'm one of those little stones near the end of the bridge, the little weird ones the masons brought along just in case they had a hole that size.

Thanks to Pete Gretsch, I'm still playing ball, but Feldspar did get a few lashes in. Before I was allowed back on the field, they made me sign a piece of paper promising to quit investigations, under penalty of immediate termination from Major League Baseball. In effect, they were asking me to choose between a job that pays me a million and a half a year and one that pays me nothing. Somehow it was a tough decision. Every team in baseball has at least two setup men, a righty and a lefty, which means there are at least sixty guys out there doing exactly what I do on the mound. Sixty weird little stones. But only one of those can make your daughter's gambling debts disappear. Only one can deliver spy-cam photos of your wife dressed up as a housekeeper. Without that power, what am I? It would appear that we'll find out.

Tomorrow is a travel day—we're headed to the East Coast for a ten-game trip that will determine whether these playoff predictions are right. Three in Washington, four in New York, and a two-game interleague series in Boston. It's make-or-break time in more ways than one. September means rosters get expanded from twenty-five to forty, and the Dogs have called up a young lefty from Riverside, a kid named Jackson with a fastball in the mid-nineties and a knee-buckling change. I'm not nervous, exactly—I've survived challenges like this—but I do feel more vulnerable this year.

After tonight's win, most of the team hit the bars to show the call-ups how that part of major-league life works. I opted to come home instead, and now I'm sitting in my apartment, flipping channels, until it's late enough to go to bed without shame. I've already seen all of the evening's baseball highlights, so I turn to CNN. The anchor is talking with a reporter in Havana, a doe-eyed American Latina, who explains that the American government is considering relaxing its stance toward Cuba. Families would be able to send more money back home, and the United States may open an embassy in Havana for the first time since 1961. So far there has been no word on lifting trade sanctions. The anchor asks if there will be legal Cuban cigars in time for Christmas—a joke, from the look on his face. The reporter, who can't see the anchor, thinks he's being serious. "Maybe so, Frank," she says. "Already there is talk of amnesty for Cuban defectors, including athletes."

I'm curious how this amnesty, if it comes to pass, will affect baseball. For starters, La Loba will be put out of business. That news should make me happy. Instead, I feel a premature twinge of nostalgia for the Cuban mystique.

Around twelve-thirty, I'm thinking about turning off the TV when the intercom buzzes. I go over to the console on the wall, but I don't recognize the woman on the screen. She has close-cropped brown hair, as short as mine, and a little diamond stud in one nostril. She's wearing jeans and a San Jose Sharks T-shirt. It occurs to me that she may be a wayward Gamer Babe. A few of the Sharks rent apartments in this building during the hockey season, but this is September. Hockey doesn't start up for over a month.

I push the button to talk. "Can I help you?"

"Adcock, let me in. It's Tiff." She peers up into the camera, and then I see it: the eyes, the curve of the face. She got me again—although I'm still not sure who she's supposed to be.

A minute later, she's standing in my living room.

"I'm free, can you believe it? We got a new judge, and he pressured the feds to deal. *You're treating the accused like a member of the Islamic State,* he told them. *She's clearly no risk to society. You have a week to structure a plea or I'm dismissing the case.*"

"You took a deal."

"That's right. I had to sell the plane to cover the legal bill, but I'm free. I'm flying commercial now. Do you know what they charge to check a bag? One bag! Someone could have warned me."

"Did they make you quit styling?"

She nods. "Lifetime ban from all four major sports leagues. No contact allowed with active players, coaches, managers, or front-office personnel. I am allowed to offer advice for free, but only to amateurs. It's a bitter pill. But the lawyers say it's temporary."

How is a lifetime ban temporary? I guess that's what you get for a jet's worth of lawyers.

"Can I ask you about Will Cunningham?"

Tiff smiles. "The Fizz . . ."

"You know he fizzled out, right? He was sent back to Triple-A."

"I heard." She sounds unbothered. "These things happen, right? Didn't you get bounced a few times your rookie year?"

"Sure, but I never paid a consultant six figures to manage my look."

"Six figures! Is that what he told you?"

"That's what people say you get. Am I wrong?"

"My services are valuable, and my prices are fair."

"Are they really? Will expected results, and now he's back in the minors. How is that a good value?"

"Every client has different needs. The Fizz was a player with unquestionable talent who could not get his mind around the major-league game."

"But how did you help him? I'm no stylist, but in my opinion you made him look worse, with the bleach job, the tacky tattoo, the jewelry. . . ."

"Exactly."

"Exactly what?"

"Will Cunningham needed a kick in the ass, and I gave it to him."

"By making him look like a rapper's ghost?"

"I was also considering a sort of spray-tanned Ken-doll look, but that could have been misinterpreted as a sincere mistake."

"You wanted to make sure he'd be a laughingstock."

"He had to fail badly. That was the only way to stir up his anger. Back in Triple-A he's going to have a long dark night of the soul, or whatever you want to call it, and he'll emerge with some kind of resolution. Either he'll step up his game, or he'll quit baseball altogether."

"But what if he doesn't see it that way? Isn't it cruel to force this crisis on him?"

"Not really. It just hastens the inevitable. There are only two possible outcomes for Will Cunningham: either he is going to become a major-league player, or he's not. I'm just making it happen faster."

She walks to the window. It's a clear night. In the distance you can see the twinkling lights of bridges over the bay.

"What are you going to do now?" I ask.

"Well, I took my niece's advice and started a channel on YouTube."

"Really?"

"Adcock! I don't know what's next. Honestly, I was hoping you could help me figure it out." She walks toward me, pooching her lips like a pinup. Her breasts swell beneath the black-and-teal shark. I can't tell if she's serious.

"I don't understand you, Tiff."

"Of course you do. We're two of a kind."

"How do you figure?"

"We're both exhausted, lonely, and banned from the work we love."

She steps close and lets the back of her hand brush the front of my jeans. "There you go," she says.

I've been on my best behavior since the shit went down in the skybox. Don't get me wrong: I'm hungry for it, and Tiff showing up here so late at night is something of a gift. But there are strings attached, I'm sure.

"Who are you supposed to be?" I ask.

"What do you mean?"

"I feel like I don't get the joke."

"The joke?"

"Yeah, all this." I point to the hair, the T-shirt. "First you were a field reporter, then you dressed up like Connie. . . . The last time we saw each other, you were a suicide blonde with an electronic cigarette. What's the costume this time?"

Tiff frowns. "This isn't a costume, Johnny. This is me."

# Acknowledgments

I am deeply grateful to my editor, Rob Bloom, for his help with this manuscript and his ongoing enthusiasm for the Adcock series. Thank you, Rob, for pushing me to do my best work and for reminding me what a privilege it is to explore baseball through Adcock's eyes.

Thanks also to my agent, Jennifer Carlson, who is nothing like Todd Ratkiss.

Thanks to my wife for never questioning what I do for a living, even when it takes the term "fantasy baseball" to a whole new level. And thanks to my kids, who still aren't old enough to read this book.

Finally, thank you to the readers of this series. In a world where you can stream fifteen major-league games every night on your phone, you chose to read a novel about a relief pitcher on a made-up team. I started writing these books because I wanted to get closer to the game than TV could take me. I wanted to go beyond the postgame interviews, beyond the press conferences, into the hidden world of pro baseball. I didn't know if anyone would join me there, but you did. Thanks for reading.

# About the Author

T. T. MONDAY is the pseudonym of novelist Nick Taylor, author of *The Disagreement* and *Father Junípero's Confessor*. *Double Switch* is his second novel to feature Johnny Adcock, after *The Setup Man*. Follow him on Twitter @ttmonday.